EDGAR ALLEN POE'S
LOST TALES

EDGAR ALLEN POE'S LOST TALES

Morgue and Mystery Stories

COMPILED & INTRODUCED
BY PETER HAINING

the apocryphile press
BERKELEY, CA
www.apocryphile.org

apocryphile press
BERKELEY, CA

Apocryphile Press
1700 Shattuck Ave #81
Berkeley, CA 94709
www.apocryphile.org

First published in London, England
by Victor Gollancz, Ltd.
Copyright 1980 by Peter Haining.
First Apocryphile edition, 2006.

ISBN 1-933993-15-4

Printed in the United States of America

CONTENTS

ACKNOWLEDGEMENTS

The Editor is deeply grateful to those who helped him in the research of this book, in particular the staff at the British Museum, the New York Public Library, and the London Library. Thanks also to Bill Lofts for assistance, Robert Haining for his contribution, and A. M. Heath Literary Agency for permission to reprint the Poe story, "The Lighthouse", completed by Robert Bloch.

INTRODUCTION

The Pioneer of Mystery

IN THE YEAR 1835, Edgar Allan Poe, struggling hard to make his impact on American literature, confided in a letter to a friend the methods he was using in the creation of the short stories he hoped might someday secure him a reputation. "The ludicrous," he said, "is heightened into the grotesque; the fearful coloured into the horrible; the witty exaggerated into the burlesque; the singular wrought out into the strange and the mystical."

Today, almost a century and a half later, it may seem surprising that a man of such unquestioned genius could have failed to receive the instant acknowledgement to which he was entitled. Yet, as we also know, while his times treated him badly, history has subsequently lauded his name and his works, seeing him clearly as a great pioneer of mystery fiction.

The Creator of the Modern Horror Story. The Developer of Science Fiction. The Father of Detective Fiction. Such laurels can, with every justification, be attached to Poe's name. Even The Most Read Fantasy Writer of the Twentieth Century is not beyond him—for despite all the brilliant authors that have emerged during the past three quarters of a century, his stories remain in print year after year in virtually every language, and the best of them are anthologized repeatedly. Time has done nothing to age this work, or deprive it of the bright spark of magic that makes it immediately appealing to each new generation.

Nor has time played the trick on Poe that it has done on other great writers in the Fantasy genre: Mary Shelley (*Frankenstein*) and Bram Stoker (*Dracula*), for instance, have become over-shadowed by their monstrous creations, yet Poe remains a colossus, the variety of his work defying any such simple association. Indeed, his name has become synonymous with all that is best in the genre, and no modern writer could hope for higher praise than to be compared with him.

There are many explanations that can, and have been, offered to explain Poe's success. His originality, his style, and the masterful way he handles atmosphere and characterization have all been singled out for praise. For my part—and I can claim to have been reading and studying Poe since childhood—it is his diversity that sets him above all others. His stories take us through such a wide range of subjects, places and times; they tell us about men from different backgrounds in many extraordinary situations and transport us from the bowels of the earth to the far reaches of space. There is hardly a topic which did not attract Poe at some time during his life, and which, after he had embraced it in his fiction, was ever quite the same again. From his own sad life too, he extracted the power of his emotions to give us stories and poems that are, quite simply, unforgettable.

I have tried to reflect his diversity of talent in this anthology, which has the distinction of containing several previously uncollected items by Poe (an achievement of which, as an editor, I am naturally proud considering the multitude of editions of his works and the innumerable studies of his life), as well as a small group of stories which were directly influential on some of his best-known tales. For though his originality of conception is never in question, Poe—like any great writer—found inspiration from other sources, as Professor Burton R. Pollin has remarked in his notable study, *Discoveries in Poe* (1970). "Almost every masterpiece of literature," he writes, "reflects a variety of sources, recent and remote, major and minor, all absorbed and held by the creative spirit in a state of dynamic but subliminal flux, until the moment of conception."

The Edgar Allan Poe Bedside Companion consists of three specific groups of stories. The first section contains three short tales which Poe acknowledged reading and which later inspired important stories of his own. In the second part I have returned to print three stories by Poe which have not appeared in his Collected Works and have consequently been unavailable to readers since the last century. And thirdly, by way of rounding out the picture, I have included three items directly inspired by Poe: a famous hoax poem "The Fire-Fiend"; "The Lighthouse", a story he left unfinished at his death and which has now been completed by one of his most distinguished literary heirs, Robert Bloch; and, finally, a completely new story never published elsewhere, "The Mad Trist", based on a fascinating idea contained in perhaps the most popular of all his works. Together, I believe, this group of nine stories throws new light on the diversity of his talent as well as adding some important items to the library of Poe material. They are all splendid reading into the bargain!

However, before you begin, let me offer a little information about the background to the stories which will, I hope, enhance your appreciation and enjoyment of them.

Poe was, by his own admission, an avid reader of newspapers and magazines throughout his life, and few periodicals gave him greater pleasure than the British monthly, *Blackwood's Magazine*, to which he tried to contribute for some years and praised in a revealing essay entitled "The Psyche Zenobia" first published in the *American Museum*, November 1838. (The story was later re-titled "How to Write a Blackwood Article" and has remained under that title ever since.)

Blackwood's Magazine was founded in 1817 by an Edinburgh bookseller-turned-publisher, William Blackwood (1776–1834) and was almost certainly the first periodical in English to publish stories and poems. The excellent taste of its various editors over the years has enabled it to flourish to this day. It seems likely that Poe began reading the magazine in his childhood, for his foster father, John Allan, imported books and magazines as well as other merchandise from Britain. What is certain is that it sparked his youthful imagination and sowed the seeds which were later to flower into several remarkable stories. Two items from *Blackwood's* which in his essay about the magazine Poe specifically mentions having read, and which we can clearly see as being influential on his work, begin this collection. They are "The Buried Alive" and "The Man in the Bell".

"The Buried Alive" appeared in the October 1821 issue of *Blackwood's* and this is how Poe described the effect the story had on him in his later essay (Poe misquotes the title, but there is no doubt it is the story he has in mind): "There was 'The Dead Alive' a capital thing!—the record of a gentleman's sensations when entombed before the breath was out of his body—full of taste, terror, sentiment, metaphysics and erudition. You would have sworn that the writer had been born and brought up in a coffin."

No author is credited with "The Buried Alive" and subsequent research has failed to identify any possible writer. That Poe should have been so attracted to the story comes as no surprise, for as a child he had always been frightened of the dark, and had heard of at least two instances of premature burial. The direct result was his story "The Premature Burial", also a first-person account, which he wrote in 1844 and which has subsequently been reprinted countless times as well as being impressively filmed with Ray Milland in 1962.

Next, in his *Blackwood's* essay, Poe turns to "The Man in the Bell" which was published in the following month's issue (November 1821):

And then there was "The Man in the Bell", a paper by-the-by which I cannot sufficiently recommend to your attention. It is the history of a young person who goes to sleep under the clapper of a church bell and is awakened by its tolling for a funeral. The sound drives him mad and, accordingly, pulling out his tablets, he gives a record of his sensations. Sensations are the great things after all!

The impression this story had on Poe is further underlined by the fact that he mentioned it again in a letter to Thomas White dated 30 April 1835. Although, once again, no author's name appears on the story, it has been established that it was written by William Maginn (1794–1842) a prolific contributor to the magazine, who was born in Cork and moved to London, where he wrote stories and essays for several of the leading publications of the day.

Maginn's story inspired two important Poe works, "The Devil in the Belfry", his grotesque little yarn published in 1839, and "The Pit and the Pendulum" (1842), the popular and quite terrifying story which has never been out of print and was filmed twice, in 1912 and 1961, the later version starring Vincent Price.

The third story in this first section also comes from a Scottish magazine and aside from its direct inspiration of a Poe story, must have done much to nurture the American's obsession with doomed heroines. The story called "The Dead Daughter" was written by Henry Glassford Bell (1803–1874) and appeared in the magazine he edited, *The Edinburgh Literary Journal,* for 1 January 1831.

Bell, who has been referred to as "The Last of the Literary Sheriffs", was initially a writer and editor, but then turned to the law, ultimately becoming Sheriff of Glasgow, so denying the world of letters a rare talent. In studying the small group of stories that Bell wrote during the three year period he ran the Journal (1828–1831), I think it is possible to see that he was one of the single most important influences on Poe, and indeed in the *Dictionary of National Biography* (1885), two of his stories, "The Dead Daughter" and "The Living Mummy" are specifically cited in this context, with the remark that from them "Edgar Poe seems to have taken the hint for two of his most famous fantasies." The Poe stories are, of course, "Morella" (1835), perhaps the most tragic of his ill-fated ladies, and the grimly humorous "Some Words with a Mummy" (1845).

The second section of the anthology includes three previously uncollected stories by Poe: "A Dream", "The Journal of Julius Rodman" and "Who is the Murderer?". While the first is just a brief, imaginative fantasy—nonetheless important—the other two are novella length: a story of travel and high adventure in unexplored regions, and the exposition of a baffling murder mystery.

"A Dream" was first recorded by Professor Killis Campbell while researching Poe and his life, but although he mentions the story in his book, *The Mind of Poe* (1933), it is not reprinted. The fantasy originally appeared in the Philadelphia *Saturday Evening Post* of 13 August 1831, and although not the earliest of his stories, is certainly one of his first attempts at fantasy fiction. It has been suggested that an eclipse of the moon on 12 February 1831, which Poe observed, may have inspired him to write the tale; but what is certain is that the employment of a dream as the basis of the fantasy was a technique he was to use again during his career.

"The Journal of Julius Rodman" shows us a completely different side of Poe's genius: that of travelogue writer. The story was written as a serial in 1840 for *Burton's Magazine*, and remains unfinished because Poe apparently quarrelled with his employer and was discharged from his job before he could complete it. Edward H. Davidson is one of the few Poe scholars to have pointed out the significance of the tale in his *Poe: a Critical Study* (1957):

> Only twice did Poe try his hand at a sustained narrative, first in "The Narrative of A. Gordon Pym" (in two instalments in the *Southern Literary Messenger* for January and February 1837, and separately as a "finished" book in 1838) and, second, in "The Journal of Julius Rodman" published serially in *Burton's Gentleman's Magazine* from January through June 1840. *The latter has never been printed separately or gathered among his tales.* [My italics.]
>
> In a way one narrative is a commentary on the other; both begin at the same place in the creative imagination—with the facts of a voyage or a journey to unexplored lands. One remains earthbound and text-confined to its sources, which Poe quite ruthlessly copied, extracted or revised; the other, "Pym", takes off from its sources, comes back to them for supporting details, and then transforms and makes them into art.
>
> In their way both are hoaxes; they presume to recount adventures with a complete, an almost deadly seriousness,

and base the separate incidents on undoubted facts which science and exploration could confirm. For "Rodman" Poe relied almost entirely on Washington Irving's *Astoria*, itself a derivation from other narratives, and on the journals of Lewis and Clark . . .

Poe calls the "Journal", "a journey beyond the extreme bounds of civilization" and goes on to add:

Within the limits of the United States there is very little ground which has not, of late years, been traversed by men of science, or the adventurer. But in those wide and desolate regions which lie north of our territory, and to the westward of Mackenzie's River, the foot of no civilized man, with the exception of Mr Rodman and his very small party, has ever been known to tread.

The central character of the story, Julius Rodman, is a typical Poe hero, a man of morbid sensibilities driven to the wilds to avoid the rest of mankind. He is said to belong to a family who had emigrated from England, lives a hermit-like existence in Kentucky, and sets off in 1791 on the expedition which is detailed in the Journal. Poe claims that the manuscript on which the account is based was "always supposed to have been lost" but has lately been rediscovered "in a secret drawer of a bureau which had belonged to Mr Julius Rodman".

The only disappointing fact about this remarkable novella, with its colourful and descriptive account of life in the American wilds —complete with dramatic encounters with dangerous animals and war-like Red Indians—is that Poe never returned to the task of completing it. This said, it still makes fascinating reading, and I am delighted to be returning it to print after such a long absence.

The last story in the section, "Who is the Murderer?", is the subject of some controversy as to whether Poe actually wrote it. The renowned Poe scholar Mary E. Phillips, in her book *Edgar Allan Poe: the Man* (1926) has no doubt in assigning it to him, and believes it was one of the articles which he said he had written for British magazines in the early 1840s. It appeared anonymously in *Blackwood's* of May 1842—the magazine we know Poe admired and to which he always wanted to contribute.

If this claim is correct (and I find the evidence convincing) then Poe wrote "Who is the Murderer?" not long after his pioneer detective story, "The Murders in the Rue Morgue" (1841), and before "The Mystery of Marie Roget", which was published between November 1842 and February 1843. This fact established, it appeared at a time when Poe was deeply absorbed with the art of "ratiocination" (as he called detective work), and the style of presentation, with the witnesses giving their testimony one by one, is very like that adopted in "The Murders in the Rue Morgue". The entire story also has much of Poe's circumstantiality, and I am sure the reader will be fascinated by the mystery whether or not he has doubts about its authorship.

In the last section of the book I have included three items inspired by Poe. Two of these are stories, but the first is a poem, "The Fire-Fiend", for of course Poe also left his mark on poetry with such marvellous verses as "The City in the Sea", "The Bells" and his immortal "The Raven".

"The Fire-Fiend" was first published some ten years after Poe's death in the *New York Saturday Press* on 19 November 1859, announced as "a recently discovered Poe manuscript". It was however prefaced by these remarks from the Editor: "We postpone several articles this week to make place for the following communication, which we print with the single remark that we 'don't see it.' " Such was the public acclaim which greeted the poem that the editor's undoubted scepticism about the authenticity of the work was ignored, and it was soon being republished in both magazine and book form as "an unpublished manuscript of the late Edgar A. Poe".

The most extraordinary part of the drama was still to be played out. For when a young Philadelphian named Charles Desmarais Gardette (1830–1884) came forward to confess that the editor's misgivings had been fully justified and that he had written the poem, hardly anyone took any notice! He had created "The Fire-Fiend", Gardette said, to prove to a friend that it was possible to imitate Poe's style and he had taken "The Raven" as his model. The subsequent widespread republication of the hoax poem only proved how right he had been.

In 1864, Gardette felt compelled to publish a booklet explaining just how he had written the poem, thereby hoping to quash once and for all the stories that it was genuine. He concluded the work with these remarks:

"The Fire-Fiend", then, was written as a hoax, published as hoax with an editorial remark sufficiently indicating the fact to any reader of fair perspicacity; and, as no money was asked, nor received for or by its publication, and no efforts whatever made to disseminate or perpetuate the hoax, either by its publisher or author, I feel no hesitation in pronouncing it, and in believing that my readers will pronounce it, to have been a venial and harmless literary joke, instead of an "unjustifiable fraud", "forgery" and a "great wrong" as some have declared it to be.

Even after such an unqualified admission, it is still the fact that over the intervening years there have been other writers and scholars who have suggested that "The Fire-Fiend" was, after all, a genuine piece by Poe. The reader will easily appreciate how this fine poem can engender such a viewpoint—but the fact remains that it *is* a fraud!

"The Lighthouse", the story which follows the poem, is undeniably partly the work of Poe, for the manuscript which was left unfinished at the time of his death still exists, and following its rediscovery was completed by Robert Bloch in 1953. The rediscovery was made by the leading Poe scholar, Professor T. O. Mabbott, who reprinted the fragment in the antiquarian journal, *Notes & Queries* of 25 April 1942. He described the work as "probably the last story Poe wrote", consisting of four pages of manuscript "written in the very neat hand characteristic of Poe's last years'' (See the sample lines at the foot of this page). Of the story itself, Professor Mabbott writes:

> Obviously the story is a typical one, finding a close parallel in theme to ''The Descent into the Maelstrom'' which also concerns an adventure with perils of the sea. The theme of loneliness is one frequent in Poe's poems and tales. Even the name of the big dog, Neptune, Poe had used for a canine character before, in his ''Julius Rodman''. And the tale was obviously to be of mood, the mood of terror. The question remains, however, which is always asked of an unfinished story. Can we guess how it would come out?

Professor Mabbott decided to invite Robert Bloch, an acknowledged master of macabre fiction and an admirer of Poe, to write his own version of the ending based on the clues existing in the manuscript. What he produced is reprinted here, and when I sought Bob's agreement to the use of the story in this collection, he re-emphasized how he had tried to retain the style and intentions of Poe's original, disguising as much as possible where he

Jan 1 — 1796. This day — my first on the light-house — I make this entry in my Diary, as agreed on with De Grät. As regularly as I can keep the journal, I will — but there is no telling what may happen to a man all alone as I am — I may get sick, or worse . . . . .

had taken over. I invite you, therefore, to try and see if you can spot where the pens changed hands before all is revealed at the end of the story. "The Lighthouse" is surely a most remarkable work by two masters of the genre whose collaboration spans the grave and almost one hundred years of time!

Collaboration is also a factor in the final story in the collection, "The Mad Trist". It was inspired by "The Fall of the House of Usher", which is widely considered to be Poe's finest short story —and also happens to be my favourite. It was while re-reading the tale recently that I had the idea for the story which my brother, Robert Haining, has worked out as "The Mad Trist".

What intrigued me once again was the reference to the "antique volume" called *The Mad Trist* by Sir Launcelot Canning which is found on the shelves in Roderick Usher's library. Passages from this book form part of the narrative of the tale, and at first reading it is easy enough to believe the work might be genuine. In fact, it is an imaginary book created by Poe, although the author is surely meant to be related to the famous William Canynge (1399–1474) the Mayor of Bristol and hero of Thomas Chatterton's Rowley Poems, which Poe so loved. Another interesting point about this Launcelot Canning is that Poe also used his name as the "author" of a piece of poetry he was going to use as the motto for a magazine *The Stylus* which he and Thomas Cottrell Clarke tried to launch in 1843. (Sadly, the plan never came to fruition.) Poe himself designed the front cover of the magazine— illustrated overleaf—as well as the motto which ran:

> —unbending that all men
> Of thy firm TRUTH may say—"Lo! this is writ
> With the antique iron pen."
> Launcelot Canning

It was as a result of this, that the names of Poe and Canning and *The Mad Trist* began to swirl around in my mind until the plot of a story took shape, inspired by Poe's invention. Once I had worked out the intriguing possibilities of the concept, I asked my brother, an accomplished writer in the fantasy field, to put some flesh on my skeleton and give it a life of its own. I hope you will agree after reading "The Mad Trist" that he has produced a story Poe himself would have approved of; read in conjunction with "The Fall of the House of Usher" it becomes doubly effective.

These, then, are my "Morgue and Mystery Tales" as Poe might have called them. Each, I think, brings us a little closer to understanding the enigma that was Edgar Allan Poe. But it is, perhaps, his destiny to be always out there in the darkness of the imagination. For should we ever find him and learn his great secret, would any fascination remain in stories such as these?

PETER HAINING
FEBRUARY, 1980

THE

STYLUS

A

Monthly Journal of Literature Proper The Fine Arts And The Drama.

Aureus aliquando STYLUS, ferreus aliquando.

Pauus Jovius.

EDITED BY

EDGAR A. POE

THE DEAD ALIVE

Anonymous

I HAD BEEN for some time ill of a low and lingering fever. My strength gradually wasted, but the sense of life seemed to become more and more acute as my corporeal powers became weaker. I could see by the looks of the doctor that he despaired of my recovery; and the soft and whispering sorrow of my friends taught me that I had nothing to hope.

One day towards the evening, the crisis took place. I was seized with a strange and indescribable quivering—a rushing sound was in my ears—I saw around my couch innumerable strange faces; they were bright and visionary, and without bodies. There was light, and solemnity, and I tried to move, but could not. For a short time a terrible confusion overwhelmed me, and when it passed off, all my recollection returned with the most perfect distinctness, but the power of motion had departed. I heard the sound of weeping at my pillow—and the voice of the nurse say, "He is dead." I cannot describe what I felt at these words. I exerted my utmost power of volition to stir myself, but I could not move even an eyelid. After a short pause my friend drew near; and sobbing, and convulsed with grief, drew his hand over my face, and closed my eyes. The world was then darkened, but I still could hear, and feel, and suffer.

When my eyes were closed, I heard by the attendants that my friend had left the room and, I soon after found, the undertakers were preparing to habit me in the garments of the grave. Their thoughtlessness was more awful than the grief of my friends. They laughed at one another as they turned me from side to side, and treated what they believed a corpse, with the most appalling ribaldry.

When they had laid me out, these wretches retired, and the

degrading formality of affected mourning commenced. For three days, a number of friends called to see me. I heard them, in low accents, speak of what I was; and more than one touched me with his finger. On the third day, some of them talked of the smell of corruption in the room.

The coffin was procured—I was lifted and laid in. My friend placed my head on what was deemed its last pillow, and I felt his tears drop on my face.

When all who had any peculiar interest in me, had for a short time looked at me in the coffin, I heard them retire; and the undertaker's men placed the lid on the coffin, and screwed it down. There were two of them present—one had occasion to go away before the task was done. I heard the fellow who was left begin to whistle as he turned the screw-nails; but he checked himself, and completed the work in silence.

I was then left alone—everyone shunned the room. I knew, however, that I was not yet buried; and though darkened and motionless, I had still hope; but this was not permitted long. The day of interment arrived—I felt the coffin lifted and borne away —I heard and felt it placed in the hearse. There was a crowd of people around; some of them spoke sorrowfully of me. The hearse began to move—I knew that it carried me to the grave. It halted, and the coffin was taken out. I felt myself carried on shoulders of men, by the inequality of the motion. A pause ensued —I heard the cords of the coffin moved—I felt it swing as dependent by them. It was lowered, and rested on the bottom of the grave—the cords were dropped upon the lid—I heard them fall. Dreadful was the effort I then made to exert the power of action, but my whole frame was immovable.

Soon after, a few handfuls of earth were thrown upon the coffin. Then there was another pause—after which the shovel was employed, and the sound of the rattling mould, as it covered me, was far more tremendous than thunder. But I could make no effort. The sound gradually became less and less, and by a surging reverberation in the coffin, I knew that the grave was filled up, and that the sexton was treading in the earth, slapping the grave with the flat of his spade. This too ceased, and then all was silent.

I had no means of knowing the lapse of time; and the silence continued. This is death, thought I, and I am doomed to remain in the earth till the resurrection. Presently the body will fall into corruption, and the epicurean worm, that is only satisfied with the flesh of man, will come to partake of the banquet that has been prepared for him with so much solicitude and care. In the contemplation of this hideous thought, I heard a low and under-sound in the earth over me, and I fancied that the worms and the reptiles of death were coming—that the mole and the rat of the grave would soon be upon me. The sound continued to grow louder and nearer. Can it be possible, I thought, that my friends suspect they have buried me too soon? The hope was truly like light bursting through the gloom of death.

The sound ceased, and presently I felt the hands of some dreadful being working about my throat. They dragged me out of the coffin by the head. I felt again the living air, but it was piercingly cold; and I was carried swiftly away—I thought to judgment, perhaps perdition.

When borne to some distance, I was then thrown down like a clod—it was not upon the ground. A moment after I found myself on a carriage; and, by the interchange of two or three brief sentences, I discovered that I was in the hands of two of those robbers who live by plundering the grave, and selling the bodies of parents, and children, and friends. One of the men sung snatches and scraps of obscene songs, as the cart rattled over the pavement of the streets.

When it halted, I was lifted out, and I soon perceived, by the closeness of the air, and the change of temperature, that I was carried into a room; and, being rudely stripped of my shroud, was placed naked on a table. By the conversation of the two fellows with the servant who admitted them, I learnt that I was that night to be dissected.

My eyes were still shut, I saw nothing; but in a short time I heard, by the bustle in the room, that the students of anatomy were assembling. Some of them came round the table, and examined me minutely. They were pleased to find that so good a subject had been procured. The demonstrator himself at last came in.

Previous to beginning the dissection, he proposed to try on me some galvanic experiment—and an apparatus was arranged for that purpose. The first shock vibrated through all my nerves: they rung and jangled like the strings of a harp. The students expressed their admiration at the convulsive effect. The second shock threw my eyes open, and the first person I saw was the doctor who had attended me. But still I was as dead: I could, however, discover among the students the faces of many with whom I was familiar; and when my eyes were opened, I heard my name pronounced by several of the students, with an accent of awe and compassion, and a wish that it had been some other subject.

When they had satisfied themselves with the galvanic phenomena, the demonstrator took the knife, and pierced me on the bosom with the point. I felt a dreadful crackling, as it were, throughout my whole frame—a convulsive shuddering instantly followed, and a shriek of horror rose from all present. The ice of death was broken up—my trance ended. The utmost exertions were made to restore me, and in the course of an hour I was in the full possession of all my faculties.

THE MAN IN THE BELL

William Maginn

IN MY YOUNGER days, bell-ringing was much more in fashion among the young men of ——, than it is now. Nobody, I believe, practises it there at present except the servants of the church, and the melody has been much injured in consequence. Some fifty years ago, about twenty of us who dwelt in the vicinity of the Cathedral, formed a club, which used to ring every peal that was called for; and, from continual practice and a rivalry which arose between us and a club attached to another steeple, and which tended considerably to sharpen our zeal, we became very Mozarts on our favourite instruments. But my bell-ringing practice was shortened by a singular accident, which not only stopped my performance, but made even the sound of a bell terrible to my ears.

One Sunday, I went with another into the belfry to ring for noon prayers, but the second stroke we had pulled showed us that the clapper of the bell we were at was muffled. Someone had been buried that morning, and it had been prepared, of course, to ring a mournful note. We did not know of this, but the remedy was easy. "Jack," said my companion, "step up to the loft, and cut off the hat," for the way we had of muffling was by tying a piece of an old hat, or of cloth (the former was preferred) to one side of the clapper, which deadened every second toll. I complied, and mounting into the belfry, crept as usual into the bell, where I began to cut away. The hat had been tied on in some more complicated manner than usual, and I was perhaps three or four minutes in getting it off; during which time my companion below was hastily called away, by a message from his sweetheart I believe, but that is not material to my story. The person who called him was a brother of the club who, knowing that the time had come for ringing for service, and not thinking that anyone was above, began to pull. At this moment I was just getting out, when I felt the bell moving; I guessed the reason at once—it was a moment of terror; but by a hasty, and almost convulsive effort, I succeeded in jumping down, and throwing myself on the flat of my back under the bell.

The room in which it was, was little more than sufficient to contain it, the bottom of the bell coming within a couple of feet of the floor of lath. At that time I certainly was not so bulky as I am now, but as I lay it was within an inch of my face. I had not laid myself down a second, when the ringing began—it was a dreadful situation. Over me swung an immense mass of metal, one touch of which would have crushed me to pieces; the floor under me was principally composed of crazy laths, and if they gave way, I was precipitated to the distance of about fifty feet upon a loft, which would, in all probability, have sunk under the impulse of my fall, and sent me to be dashed to atoms upon the marble floor of the chancel, an hundred feet below. I remembered—for fear is quick in recollection—how a common clock-wright, about a month before, had fallen, and bursting through the floors of the steeple, driven in the ceilings of the porch, and even broken into the marble tombstone of a bishop who slept beneath. This was my first terror, but the ringing had not continued a minute, before a more awful and immediate dread came on me. The deafening sound of the bell smote into my ears with a thunder which made me fear their drums would crack. There was not a fibre of my body it did not thrill through: it entered my very soul; thought and reflection were almost utterly banished; I only retained the sensation of agonizing terror. Every moment I saw the bell sweep within an inch of my face; and my eyes—I could not close them, though to look at the object was bitter as death—followed it instinctively in its oscillating progress until it came back again. It was in vain I said to myself that it could come no nearer at any future swing than it did at first; every time it descended, I endeavoured to shrink into the very floor to avoid being buried under the down-sweeping mass; and then reflecting on the danger of pressing too weightily on my frail support, would cower up again as far as I dared.

At first my fears were mere matter of fact. I was afraid the pulleys above would give way, and let the bell plunge on me. At another time, the possibility of the clapper being shot out in some sweep, and dashing through my body, as I had seen a ramrod glide through a door, flitted across my mind. The dread also, as I have already mentioned, of the crazy floor tormented me, but these soon gave way to fears not more unfounded, but more visionary, and of course more tremendous. The roaring of the bell confused my intellect, and my fancy soon began to teem with all sorts of strange and terrifying ideas. The bell pealing above, and opening its jaws with a hideous clamour, seemed to me at one time a ravening monster, raging to devour me; at another, a whirlpool ready to suck me into its bellowing abyss. As I gazed on it, it assumed all shapes; it was a flying eagle, or rather a roc of the Arabian story-tellers, clapping its wings and scream-ing over me. As I looked upward into it, it would appear some-times to lengthen into indefinite extent, or to be twisted at the end into the spiral folds of the tail of a flying-dragon. Nor was the flaming breath, or fiery glance of that fabled animal, wanting to complete the picture. My eyes inflamed, bloodshot and glaring, invested the supposed monster with a full proportion of unholy light.

It would be endless were I to merely hint at all the fancies that possessed my mind. Every object that was hideous and roaring presented itself to my imagination. I often thought that I was in a hurricane at sea, and that the vessel in which I was embarked tossed under me with the most furious vehemence. The air, set in motion by the swinging of the bell, blew over me, nearly with the violence, and more than the thunder of a tempest; and the floor seemed to reel under me, as under a drunken man. But the most awful of all the ideas that seized on me were drawn from the supernatural. In the vast cavern of the bell hideous faces appeared, and glared down on me with terrify-ing frowns, or with grinning mockery, still more appalling. At last, the devil himself, accoutred, as in the common description of the evil spirit, with hoof, horn, and tail, and eyes of infernal lustre, made his appearance, and called on me to curse God and worship him, who was powerful to save me. This dread suggestion he uttered with the full-toned clangour of the bell. I had him within an inch of me, and I thought on the fate of the Santon Barsisa. Strenuously and desperately I defied him, and bade him be gone. Reason, then, for a moment, resumed her sway, but it was only to fill me with fresh terror, just as the lightning dispels the gloom that surrounds the benighted mariner, but to show him that his vessel is driving on a rock, where she must inevitably be dashed to pieces. I found I was becoming delirious, and trembled lest reason should utterly desert me. This is at all times an agonizing thought, but it smote me then with tenfold agony. I feared lest, when utterly deprived of my senses, I should rise, to do which I was every moment tempted by that strange feeling which calls on a man, whose head is dizzy from standing on the battlement of a lofty castle, to precipitate himself from it, and then death would be instant and tremendous. When I thought of this, I became desperate. I caught the floor with a grasp which drove the blood from my nails; and I yelled with the cry of despair. I called for help, I prayed, I shouted, but all the efforts of my voice were, of course, drowned in the bell. As it passed over my mouth, it occasionally echoed my cries, which mixed not with its own sound, but preserved their distinct character. Perhaps this was but fancy. To me, I know, they then sounded as if they were the shouting, howling, or laughing of the fiends with which my imagination had peopled the gloomy cave which swung over me.

You may accuse me of exaggerating my feelings; but I am not. Many a scene of dread have I since passed through, but they are nothing to the self-inflicted terrors of this half hour. The ancients have doomed one of the damned, in their Tartarus, to lie under a rock, which every moment seems to be descending to annihilate him—and an awful punishment it would be. But if to this you add a clamour as loud as if ten thousand furies were howling about you—a deafening uproar banishing reason, and driving you to madness—you must allow that the bitterness of the pang was rendered more terrible. There is no man, firm as his nerves may be, who could retain his courage in this situation.

In twenty minutes the ringing was done. Half of that time passed over me without power of computation—the other half appeared an age. When it ceased, I became gradually more quiet, but a new fear retained me. I knew that five minutes would elapse without ringing but, at the end of that short time, the bell would be rung a second time, for five minutes more. I could not calculate time. A minute and an hour were of equal duration. I feared to rise, lest the five minutes should have elapsed, and the ringing be again commenced, in which case I should be crushed, before I could escape, against the walls or framework of the bell. I therefore still continued to lie down, cautiously shifting myself, however, with a careful gliding, so that my eye no longer looked into the hollow. This was of itself a considerable relief. The cessation of the noise had, in a great measure, the effect of stupefying me, for my attention, being no longer occupied by the chimeras I had conjured up, began to flag. All that now distressed me was the constant expectation of the second ringing, for which, however, I settled myself with a kind of stupid resolution. I closed my eyes, and clenched my teeth as firmly as if they were screwed in a vice. At last the dreaded moment came, and the first swing of the bell extorted a groan from me, as they say the most resolute victim screams at the sight of the rack, to which he is for a second time destined. After this, however, I lay silent and lethargic, without a thought. Wrapped in the defensive armour of stupidity, I defied the bell and its intonations. When it ceased, I was roused a little by the hope of escape. I did not, however, decide on this step hastily but, putting up my hand with the utmost caution, I touched the rim. Though the ringing had ceased, it still was tremulous from the sound, and shook under my hand, which instantly recoiled as from an electric jar. A quarter of an hour probably elapsed before I again dared to make the experiment, and then I found it at rest. I determined to lose no time, fearing that I might have lain then already too long, and that the bell for evening service would catch me. This dread stimulated me, and I slipped out with the utmost rapidity, and arose. I stood, I suppose, for a minute, looking with silly wonder on the place of my imprisonment, penetrated with joy at escaping, but then rushed down the stony and irregular stair with the velocity of lightning, and arrived in the bellringer's room. This was the last act I had power to accomplish. I leant against the wall, motionless and deprived of thought, in which posture my companions found me when, in the course of a couple of hours, they returned to their occupation.

They were shocked, as well they might be, at the figure before them. The wind of the bell had excoriated my face, and my dim and stupefied eyes were fixed with a lack-lustre gaze in my raw eyelids. My hands were torn and bleeding, my hair dishevelled, and my clothes tattered. They spoke to me, but I gave no answer. They shook me, but I remained insensible. They then became alarmed, and hastened to remove me. He who had first gone up with me in the forenoon, met them as they carried me through the churchyard, and through him, who was shocked at having, in some measure, occasioned the accident, the cause of my misfortune was discovered. I was put to bed at home, and remained for three days delirious, but gradually recovered my senses. You may be sure the bell formed a prominent topic of my ravings, and if I heard a peal, they were instantly increased to the utmost violence. Even when the delirium abated, my sleep was continually disturbed by imagined ringings, and my dreams were haunted by the fancies which almost maddened me while in the steeple. My friends removed me to a house in the country, which was sufficiently distant from any place of worship, to save me from the apprehensions of hearing the church-going bell; for what Alexander Selkirk, in Cowper's poem, complained of as a misfortune, was then to me as a blessing. Here I recovered; but, even long after recovery, if a gale wafted the notes of a peal towards me, I started with nervous apprehension. I felt a Mahometan hatred to all the bell tribe, and envied the subjects of the Commander of the Faithful the sonorous voice of their

Muezzin. Time cured this, as it does the most of our follies; but, even at the present day, if, by chance, my nerves be unstrung, some particular tones of the cathedral bell have power to surprise me into a momentary start.

THE DEAD DAUGHTER

Henry Glassford Bell

THE BUILDING WAS a solitary one, and had a cold and forbidding aspect. Its tenant, Adolphus Walstein, was a man whom few liked: not that they charged him with any crime, but he was of an unsocial temperament; and ever since he came to the neighbourhood, thinly inhabited as it was, he had contracted no friendship, formed no acquaintance. He seemed fond of wandering among the mountains; and his house stood far up in one of the wild valleys formed by the Rhaetian Alps, which intersect Bohemia.

He was married, and his wife had once been beautiful. She even yet bore the traces of that beauty, though somewhat faded. She must have been of high birth too, for her features and gait were patrician. She spoke little; but you could not look on her and fancy that her silence was for lack of thought.

They had one only child—a daughter—a pale but beautiful girl. She was very young—not yet in her teens—but the natural mirth of childhood characterized her not. It seemed as if the gloom that had settled round her parents had affected her too; it seemed as if she had felt the full weight of their misfortunes, almost before she could have known what misfortune was. She smiled sometimes, but very faintly; yet it was a lovely smile—more lovely that it was melancholy. She was not strong; there was in her limbs none of the glowing vigour of health. She cared not for sporting in the fresh breeze on the hillside. If ever she gathered wild flowers, it was only to bring them home, to lay them in her mother's lap, and wreathe them into withered garlands.

Much did they love that gentle child: they had nothing else in the wide world to love, save an old domestic, and a huge Hungarian dog. Yet it was evident Paulina could not live; at least her life was a thing of uncertainty—of breathless hope and fear. She was tall beyond her years; but she was fragile as the stalk of the white-crowned lily. She was very like her mother; though there was at times a shade upon her brow that reminded you strongly of the darker countenance of her father. It was said, that when he took his gun, and went out all day in search of the red deer, far up among the rocky heights, he would forget his purpose for hours, and seating himself upon some Alpine promontory, would gaze upon his lonely house in the valley below, till the sun went down in the stormy west; and as evening drew on, and a single light faintly glimmered from one of the windows of his mansion, he has brushed a hot tear from his eye, and started into recollection. It was dark ere he came home, and the winds howled drearily. In their sitting room—a room but barely furnished—he found his wife plying her needle beside the lamp, and at a little distance the dying flame of the wood fire threw its ghastly flickerings on the pale face of his daughter. He stood at the door, and leant upon his gun in silence. They knew his mood, and were silent also. His eye was fixed upon his daughter; she would have fascinated yours too. *It was no common countenance.* Not that any individual feature could have been singled out as peculiar, but the general expression was such as, once seen, haunted the memory for ever. Perhaps it was the black eye—blacker than the ebon hair—contrasted with the deadly paleness of her white-rose cheek. It was deep sunk, too, under her brow. But it is needless to form conjectures: none knew in what that expression originated—there was a mystery in it. She had a long thin arm, and tapering fingers, and a hand crossed by many a blue vein. Its touch was in general thrillingly cold, yet at times it was feverishly hot. Her mother had borne many a child, but all died in early infancy. Yet her father's fondest wish was to see a son rising by his side into manhood; nor did he despair of having the wish gratified. It was said his dying commands would have given that son much to do.

Paulina was now thirteen; but the canker was busy within, and even her mother saw at last that she, too, was to be taken from her. It was a stern dispensation; the only child of her heart—the only one whom her sleepless care had been able to fence in from the grasp of the spoiler—her meditation and her dream for thirteen years—the one only sad sunbeam whose watery and uncertain ray lighted up their solitude. But evil had followed them as a doom, nor was that doom yet completed.

She died upon an autumn evening. She had been growing weaker for many a day, and they saw it, but spoke not of it. Nor did she; it seemed almost a pain for her to speak; and when she did, it was in a low soft tone, inaudible almost to all but the ear of affection. Yet was the mind within her busy with all the restless activity of feverish reverie. She had strange daydreams; and life and the distant world often flashed upon her in far more than the brightness of reality. Often, too, all faded away; and though her eyes were still open, darkness fell around her, and she dwelt among the mysteries and immaterial shapes of some shadowy realm. It would be fearful to know all that passed in the depth of that lonely girl's spirit. It was an autumn evening—sunny, but not beautiful—silent, but not serene. She had walked to the brook that came down the mountains, and which formed a pool and babbling cascade not a stone-cast from the door. Perhaps she grew suddenly faint; for her mother, who stood at the window, saw her coming more hastily than usual across the field. She went to meet her; she was within arm's length, when her daughter gave a faint moan, and, falling forward, twined her cold arms round her mother's neck, and looked up into her face with a look of agony. It was only for a moment; her dark eye became fixed—it grew white with the whiteness of death, and the mother carried her child's body into its desolate home.

If her father wept—it was at night when there was no eye to see. The Hungarian dog howled over the dead body of its young mistress, and the old domestic sat by the unkindled hearth, and wept as for her own firstborn; but the father loaded his gun, as was his wont, and went away among the mountains.

The priests came, and the coffin, and a few of the simple peasants. She was carried forth from her chamber, and her father followed. The procession winded down the valley. The tinkling of the holy bell mingled sadly with the funeral chant. At last the little train disappeared; for the churchyard was among the hills, some miles distant. The mother was left alone. She fell upon her knees, and lifted up her eyes and her clasped hands to her God, and prayed—fervently prayed, from the depths of her soul—that he might never curse her with another child. The prayer was almost impious; but she was frantic in her deep despair, and we dare not judge her.

A year has passed away, and that lonely house is still in the Bohemian valley, and its friendless inmates haunt it still. Walstein's wife bears him another child, and hope almost beats again in his bosom, as he asks, with somewhat of a father's pride, if he has now a son. But the child was a daughter, and his hopes were left unfulfilled. They christened the infant Paulina; and many a long day and dreary night did its mother hang over its cradle, and shed tears of bitterness, as she thought of her who lay unconscious in the churchyard away among the hills. The babe grew, but not in the rosiness of health. Yet it seldom suffered from acute pain; and when it wept, it was with a kind of suppressed grief, that seemed almost unnatural to one so young. It was long ere it could walk; when at last it did, it was without any previous effort.

Time passed on without change and without incident. Paulina was ten years old. Often had Philippa, with maternal fondness, pointed out to her husband the resemblance which she alleged existed between their surviving child and her whom they had laid in the grave. Walstein, as he listened to his wife, fixed his dark penetrating eye upon his daughter, and spoke not. The resemblance was, indeed, a striking one—it was almost supernatural. She was the same tall pale girl, with black, deep sunk eyes, and long dark ebon hair. Her arms and hands were precisely of the same mould, and they had the same thrilling coldness in their touch. Her manners, too, her disposition, the sound of her voice, her motions, her habits, and, above all, her expression of countenance—that characteristic and indescribable expression—were the very same. Her mother loved to dwell upon this resemblance; but her father, though he gazed and gazed upon her, yet ever and anon started, and walked with hasty strides across the room, and sometimes, even at night, rushed out into the darkness, as one oppressed with wild and fearful fancies.

They had few of the comforts, and none of the luxuries of life, in that Bohemian valley. Philippa had carefully laid aside all the clothes that belonged to her dead daughter; and now that the last child of her age was growing up, and was so like her that was gone, she loved to dress her sometimes in her sister's dress; and the pale child wore the clothes, and talked of the lost Paulina, almost as if she had known her.

One night her mother plied her needle beside her lamp, and at a little distance her daughter, in a simple white dress, which had once been another's, sat musing over the red embers of a dying fire. A thunderstorm was gathering, and the rain was already falling heavily. Walstein entered; his eye rested on his daughter, and he almost shrieked; but he recovered himself, and with a quivering lip sat down in a distant corner of the room. His Hungarian dog was with him; it seemed to have caught the direction of his master's eye, and as its own rested keenly on Paulina, the animal uttered a low growl. It was strange that the dog never seemed to love the child. It is probable that she was hardly aware of her father's entrance, for she appeared absorbed in her own thoughts. As the blue and flickering flame fell upon her face, she smiled faintly.

"O God! it is! it is!" cried Walstein, and fell senseless on the floor.

His wife and daughter hurried to his assistance, and he recovered; but he pointed to Paulina, and said falteringly, "Philippa! send *her* to bed." With a quiet step, his daughter moved across the room; at the door, she was about to kiss her mother, but Walstein thundered out, "Forbear!" and rising, closed the door with trembling violence. Philippa had often seen her husband in his wilder moods, but seldom thus strangely agitated; yet, had she known the conviction that had arisen in his mind, she would have ceased to wonder.

He had watched long and narrowly, and now he was unable to

conceal longer from himself the fearful truth. It was not in her wan beauty alone that she resembled her sister—it was not merely in the external development of her form; he knew, he felt, that the second Paulina, born after her sister's death, was *the same Paulina as she whom he had laid in the grave*. There was horror in the idea, yet could it not be resisted. But even now he breathed it not to his wife, and silently they passed to their chamber. The secret of his soul, however, which he would never have told her by day and awake, the wretched Philippa gathered from him in his unconscious mutterings in the dead watches of the night. When the thought came upon her, it fell upon her heart like a weight of lead. Her maternal affection struggled with it, and with the thousand proofs that came crowding of themselves into her memory, to strengthen and to rivet it, and the struggle almost overturned her reason.

The Paulina, in whom her heart was wrapped up twelve years ago, had frequently dreams of a mysterious meaning, which she used to repeat to her mother when no one else was by. A few days after the occurrences of the evening to which we have alluded, the living child, who had come in the place of the dead, told Philippa she had dreamt a dream. She recited it, and Philippa shuddered to hear an exact repetition of one she well remembered listening to long ago, and which she had ever since locked up in her own bosom. Even in sleep, it seemed that, by some awful mystery, Paulina was living over again.

Time still passed on, and the pale child shot up into a girl. She was thirteen; though a stranger would have thought her some years older. It was manifest that she, too, was dying. (There was a dismal doubt haunted her father's mind whether she had ever lived.) She never spoke of her deceased sister; indeed, she seldom spoke at all; but when they asked if she were well, she shook her head, and stretched an arm towards the churchyard.

To that churchyard her father went one moonlight night. It was a wild fancy, yet he resolved to open his daughter's grave, and look once more upon her mouldering remains. He had a reason for his curiosity, which he scarcely dared own even to himself. He told the sexton of his purpose; and, though the old man guessed not his object, he took his spade and his pickaxe, and speedily commenced his task. It was an uncertain night. The wind came in gusts, and sometimes died away into strange silence. The dim moonlight fell upon the white tomb-stones, and the shadows of the passing clouds glided over them like spirits. The sexton pursued his work, and had already dug deep. Walstein stood by his side.

"I have not come to the coffin yet," said the old man, in a tone bordering upon wonder; "yet I could tell the very spot blindfold in which I put it with these hands thirteen years ago."

"Dig on, for the love of Heaven!" said Walstein, and his heart began to beat audibly. There was a short pause.

"My digging is of no use," said the sexton. "I am past the place where I laid the coffin; and may the Holy Virgin protect me, for there is not a vestige either of it or the body left."

Walstein groaned convulsively, and leapt into the grave, but in vain; the sexton had reported truly. He had just stepped up again into the moonlight, when a cold hand was laid upon his shoulder. He started, and turning round, saw that his daughter stood beside him.

"Paulina! Just Heaven! what can have brought you so far from home? at night, too, and weak as you are? it will be your destruction."

She took no notice of the question, but fixing her quiet look upon the grave, she said, "Father, I shall soon lie there."

It was the thirteenth anniversary of Paulina's death, and the swollen brook was brawling hoarsely down the mountains, for a tempestuous autumn had already anticipated winter. The shutters of the upper chamber were closed, and Philippa sat by the sickbed of her last child. The sufferer raised her pale and languid head, and whilst her dark eye appeared to wander in the delirium of fever, she said, with a struggle, "Mother, is it not a mysterious imagination—but I feel as if I had lived before, and that my thoughts were happier and better than they are now?" Philippa shuddered, and gazed almost with terror upon her child. "It is a dream, Paulina; one of the waking dreams of over-watchfulness. Be still, sweet girl; an hour's sleep will refresh you." As she spoke, Paulina *did* sleep, but there was little to refresh in such slumber. Her whole frame was agitated convulsively; her bosom heaved with unnatural beating; her hands alternately grasped the coverlet, as if to tear it into shreds, and were ever and anon lifted up to her head, where her fingers twined themselves among the tresses of her ebon hair; her lips moved incessantly; her teeth chattered; her breath came short and thick, as if it would have made itself palpable to the senses. Terrible gibberings succeeded, and her poor mother knew that the moment of dissolution was at hand. In an instant all was still—the grasp of the hand was relaxed—the heaving and the beating ceased—the lips were open, but the breath of life that had ebbed and flowed between them had finished its task, and was gone; a damp distillation stood upon the brow—it was the last sign of agony which expiring nature gave.

That night Walstein dreamed a dream. Paulina, wrapped in her winding sheet, stood opposite his couch. Her face was pale and beautiful as in life, but under the folds of her shroud he discovered the hideous form of a skeleton. The vision became double: a grave opened as if spontaneously, and another Paulina burst the cerements asunder, and looked with her dead eye full upon her father. Walstein trembled, and awoke. A strange light glanced under his chamber door. Who was there stirring at that dead hour of night? He threw the curtains aside. The moon was still up; an indescribable impulse urged him to rush towards the room in which the body of his daughter lay. He passed along the lobby; the door of the chamber was open; the Hungarian dog lay dead at the threshold; *the corpse was gone*.

A DREAM

Edgar Allan Poe

A FEW EVENINGS since, I laid myself down for my night's repose. It has been a custom with me, for years past, to peruse a portion of the Scriptures before I close my eyes in the slumbers of night. I did so in the present instance. By chance, I fell upon the spot where inspiration has recorded the dying agonies of the God of Nature. Thoughts of these, and the scenes which followed his giving up the ghost, pursued me as I slept.

There is certainly something mysterious and incomprehensible in the manner in which the wild vagaries of the imagination often arrange themselves; but the solution of this belongs to the physiologist rather than the reckless dreamer.

It seemed that I was some Pharisee, returning from the scene of death. I had assisted in driving the sharpest nails through the palms of Him who hung on the cross, a spectacle of the bitterest woe that mortality ever felt. I could hear the groan that ran through his soul, as the rough iron grated on the bones when I drove it through.

I retired a few steps from the place of execution, and turned round to look at my bitterest enemy. The Nazarene was not yet dead: the life lingered in the mantle of clay, as if it shuddered to walk alone through the valley of death. I thought I could see the cold damp that settles on the brow of the dying, now standing in large drops on His. I could see each muscle quiver—the eye, that began to lose its lustre, in the hollow stare of the corpse. I could hear the low gurgle in his throat. A moment—and the chain of existence was broken, and a link dropped into eternity.

I turned away, and wandered listlessly on, till I came to the centre of Jerusalem. At a short distance rose the lofty turrets of the Temple, its golden roof reflected rays as bright as the source from which they emanated. A feeling of conscious pride stole over me, as I looked over the broad fields and lofty mountains which surrounded this pride of the eastern world. On my right rose Mount Olivet, covered with shrubbery and vineyards; beyond that, and bounding the skirts of mortal vision, appeared mountains piled on mountains; on the left were the lovely plains of Judea; and I thought it was a bright picture of human existence, as I saw the little brook Cedron speeding its way through the meadows, to the distant lake. I could hear the gay song of the beauteous maiden, as she gleaned in the distant harvest field; and, mingling with the echoes of the mountain, was heard the shrill whistle of the shepherd's pipe, as he called the wandering lamb to its fold. A perfect loveliness had thrown itself over animated nature.

But ''a change soon came o'er the spirit of my dream.'' I felt a sudden coldness creeping over me. I instinctively turned towards the sun, and saw a hand slowly drawing a mantle of crape over it. I looked for stars, but each one had ceased to twinkle—for the same hand had enveloped them in the badge of mourning. The silver light of the moon did not dawn on the sluggish waves of the Dead Sea, as they sang the hoarse requiem of the Cities of the Plain; but she hid her face, as if shuddering to look on what was doing on the earth. I heard a muttered groan, as the spirit of darkness spread his pinions over an astonished world.

Unutterable despair now seized me. I could feel the flood of life slowly rolling back to its fountain, as the fearful thought stole over me, that the day of retribution had come.

Suddenly, I stood before the Temple. The veil, which had hid its secrets from unhallowed gaze, was now rent. I looked for a moment: the priest was standing by the altar, offering up the expiatory sacrifice. The fire, which was to kindle the mangled limbs of the victim, gleamed for a moment on the distant walls, and then was lost in utter darkness. He turned around, to rekindle it from the living fire of the candlestick; but that, too, was gone. It was still as the sepulchre.

I turned and rushed into the street. The street was vacant. No sound broke the stillness, except the yell of the wild dog, who revelled on the half-burnt corpse in the Valley of Hinnom. I saw a light stream from a distant window, and made my way towards it. I looked in at the open door. A widow was preparing the last morsel she could glean for her dying babe. She had kindled a little fire; and I saw with what utter hopelessness of heart she beheld the flame sink away, like her own dying hopes.

Darkness covered the universe. Nature mourned, for its parent had died. The earth had enrobed herself in the habiliments of sorrow, and the heavens were clothed in the sables of mourning. I now roamed in restlessness, and heeded not whither I went. At once there appeared a light in the east. A column of light shot athwart the gloom, like the light-shot gleams on the darkness of the midnight of the pit, and illuminated the sober murkiness that surrounded me. There was an opening in the vast arch of heaven's broad expanse. With wondering eyes, I turned towards it.

Far into the wilderness of space, and at a distance that can only be meted by a "line running parallel with eternity", but still awfully plain and distinct, appeared the same person whom I had clothed with the mock purple of royalty. He was now garmented in the robe of the King of Kings. He sat on his throne: but it was not one of whiteness. There was mourning in heaven; for, as each angel knelt before him, I saw that the wreath of immortal amaranth which circled his brow was changed for one of cypress.

I turned to see whither I had wandered. I had come to the burial ground of the monarchs of Israel. I gazed with trembling limbs, as I saw the clods which covered the mouldering bones of some tyrant begin to move. I looked at where the last monarch had been laid, in all the splendour and pageantry of death, and the sculptured monument began to tremble. Soon it was overturned, and from it issued the tenant of the grave. It was a hideous, unearthly form, such as Dante, in his wildest flights of terrified fancy, never conjured up. I could not move, for terror had tied up volition. It approached me.

I saw the grave-worm twining itself amongst the matted locks which in part covered the rotten skull. The bones creaked on each other as they moved on the hinges, for its flesh was gone. I listened to their horrid music, as this parody on poor mortality stalked along. He came up to me; and, as he passed, he breathed the cold damps of the lonely, narrow house directly in my face.

The chasm in the heavens closed; and, with a convulsive shudder, I awoke.

THE JOURNAL OF JULIUS RODMAN
Being an Account of the First Passage across the Rocky
Mountains of North America ever Achieved by
Civilised Man

Edgar Allan Poe

I

AFTER THE DEATH of my father, and both sisters, I took no
further interest in our plantation at the Point, and sold it, at a
complete sacrifice, to M. Junôt. I had often thought of trapping
up the Missouri, and resolved now to go on an expedition up that
river, and try to procure peltries, which I was sure of being able to
sell at Petite Côte to the private agents of the Northwest Fur
Company. I believed that much more property might be acquired
in this way, with a little enterprise and courage, than I could make
by any other means. I had always been fond, too, of hunting and
trapping, although I had never made a business of either, and I
had a great desire to explore some portion of our western country,
about which Pierre Junôt had often spoken to me. He was the
eldest son of the neighbour who bought me out, and was a man of
strange manners and somewhat eccentric turn of mind, but still
one of the best-hearted fellows in the world, and certainly as
courageous a man as ever drew breath, although of no great
bodily strength. He was of Canadian descent, and having gone,
once or twice, on short excursions for the Fur Company, in which
he had acted as *voyageur*, was fond of calling himself one, and of
talking about his trips. My father had been very fond of Pierre,
and I thought a good deal of him myself; he was a great favourite,
too, with my younger sister, Jane, and I believe they would have
been married had it been God's will to have spared her.

When Pierre discovered that I had not entirely made up my

mind what course to pursue after my father's death, he urged me to fit out a small expedition for the river, in which he would accompany me; and he had no difficulty in bringing me over to his wishes. We agreed to push up the Missouri as long as we found it possible, hunting and trapping as we went, and not to return until we had secured as many peltries as would be a fortune for us both. His father made no objection and gave him about three hundred dollars; then we proceeded to Petite Côte for the purpose of getting our equipments, and raising as many men as we could for the voyage.

Petite Côte* is a small place on the north bank of the Missouri, about twenty miles from its junction with the Mississippi. It lies at the foot of a range of low hills, and upon a sort of ledge, high enough above the river to be out of the reach of the June freshets. There are not more than five or six houses, and these of wood, in the upper part of the place; but, nearer to the east, there is a chapel and twelve or fifteen good dwellings, running parallel with the river. There are about a hundred inhabitants, mostly Creoles of Canadian descent. They are extremely indolent, and make no attempt at cultivating the country around them, which is a rich soil, except now and then when a little is done in the way of gardening. They live principally by hunting, and trading with the Indians for peltries, which they sell again to the Northwest Company's agents. We expected to meet with no difficulty here in getting recruits for our journey, or equipments, but were disappointed in both particulars; for the place was too poor in every respect to furnish all that we wanted, so as to render our voyage safe and efficient.

We designed to pass through the heart of a country infested with Indian tribes, of whom we knew nothing except by vague report, and whom we had every reason to believe ferocious and treacherous. It was therefore particularly necessary that we should go well provided with arms and ammunition, as well as in some force as regards numbers; and if our voyage was to be

*Now St Charles.

a source of profit, we must take with us canoes of sufficient
capacity to bring home what peltries we might collect. It was the
middle of March when we first reached Petite Côte, and we did
not succeed in getting ready until the last of May. We had to send
twice down the river to the Point for men and supplies, and
neither could be obtained except at great cost. We should have
failed at last in getting many things absolutely requisite, if it had
not so happened that Pierre met with a party on its return from a
trip up the Mississippi, and engaged six of its best men, besides a
canoe, or piroque, purchasing, at the same time, most of the
surplus stores and ammunition.

This seasonable aid enabled us to get fairly ready for the voyage
before the first of June. On the third of this month (1791) we bade
adieu to our friends at Petite Côte, and started on our expedition.
Our party consisted in all of fifteen persons. Of these, five were
Canadians from Petite Côte, and had all been on short excursions up the river. They were good boatmen, and excellent companions, as far as singing French songs went, and drinking, at
which they were pre-eminent; although, in truth, it was a rare
thing to see any of them so far the worse for liquor as to be incapable of attending to duty. They were always in a good humour,
and always ready to work; but as hunters I did not think them
worth much, and as fighting men I soon discovered they were not
to be depended upon. There were two of these five Canadians
who engaged to act as interpreters for the first five or six hundred
miles up the river (should we proceed so far), and then we hoped
to procure an Indian occasionally to interpret, should it be necessary; but we had resolved to avoid, as far as possible, any
meetings with the Indians, and rather to trap ourselves than run
the great risk of trading, with so small a party as we numbered. It
was our policy to proceed with the greatest caution, and expose
ourselves to notice only when we could not avoid it.

The six men whom Pierre had engaged from aboard the return
Mississippi boat were as different a set from the Canadians as
could well be imagined. Five of them were brothers, by the name
of Greely (John, Robert, Meredith, Frank and Poindexter), and

bolder or finer looking persons it would have been difficult to find. John Greely was the eldest and stoutest of the five, and had the reputation of being the strongest man, as well as best shot, in Kentucky, from which State they all came. He was full six feet in height, and of most extraordinary breadth across the shoulders, with large strongly-knit limbs. Like most men of great physical strength, he was exceedingly good-tempered, and on this account was greatly beloved by us all. The other four brothers were all strong, well-built men too, although not to be compared with John. Poindexter was as tall, but very gaunt, and of a singularly fierce appearance; but, like his elder brother, he was of peaceable demeanour. All of them were experienced hunters and capital shots. They had gladly accepted Pierre's offer to go with us, and we made an arrangement with them which ensured them an equal share with Pierre and myself in the profits of the enterprise; that is to say, we divided the proceeds into three parts, one of which was to be mine, one Pierre's, and one shared among the five brothers.

The sixth man whom we enlisted from the return boat was also a good recruit. His name was Alexander Wormley, a Virginian, and a very strange character. He had originally been a preacher of the gospel, and had afterwards fancied himself a prophet, going about the country with a long beard and hair, and in his bare feet, haranguing everyone he met. This hallucination was now diverted into another channel, and he thought of nothing else than of finding gold mines in some of the fastnesses of the country. Upon this subject he was as entirely mad as any man could well be; but upon all others was remarkably sensible and even acute. He was a good boatman and a good hunter, and as brave a fellow as ever stepped, besides being of great bodily strength and swiftness of foot. I counted much upon this recruit, on account of his enthusiastic character, and in the end I was not deceived, as will appear.

Our other two recruits were a negro belonging to Pierre Junôt, named Toby, and a stranger whom we had picked up in the woods near Mill's Point, and who joined our expedition upon the instant as soon as we mentioned our design. His name was Andrew Thornton, also a Virginian, and I believe of excellent family, belonging to the Thorntons of the northern part of the State. He had been from Virginia about three years; during the whole of which time he had been rambling about the western country, with no other companion than a large dog of the Newfoundland species. He had collected no peltries, and did not seem to have any object in view, more than the gratification of a roving and adventurous propensity. He frequently amused us, when sitting around our camp fires at night, with the relation of his adventures and hardships in the wilderness, recounting them with a straightforward earnestness which left us no room to doubt their truth; although, indeed, many of them had a marvellous air. Experience afterwards taught us that the dangers and difficulties of the solitary hunter can scarcely be exaggerated, and that the real task is to depict them to the hearer in sufficiently distinct colours. I took a great liking to Thornton, from the first hour in which I saw him.

I have only said a few words respecting Toby; but he was not the least important personage of our party. He had been in old M. Junôt's family for a great number of years, and had proved himself a faithful negro. He was rather too old to accompany such an expedition as ours; but Pierre was not willing to leave him. He was an able-bodied man, however, and still capable of enduring great fatigue. Pierre himself was probably the feeblest of our whole company, as regards bodily strength, but he possessed great sagacity, and a courage which nothing could daunt. His manners were sometimes extravagant and boisterous, which led him to get into frequent quarrels, and had once or twice seriously endangered the success of our expedition; but he was a true friend, and in that one point I considered him invaluable.

I have now given a brief account of all our party, as it was when we left Petite Côte.* To carry ourselves and accoutrements, as

*Mr Rodman has not given any description of himself; and the account of his party is by no means complete without a portraiture of its leader. "He was about twenty-five years of age," says Mr James Rodman in a memorandum now before us, "when he started up the river. He was a remarkably vigorous and active man,

well as to bring home what peltries might be obtained, we had two large boats. The smallest of these was a piroque made of birch bark, sewed together with the fibres of the roots of the spruce tree, the seams payed with pine resin, and the whole so light that six men could carry it with ease. It was twenty feet long, and could be rowed with from four to twelve oars; drawing about eighteen inches water when loaded to the gunwale and, when empty, not more than ten. The other was a keel-boat which we had made at Petite Côte (the canoe having been purchased by Pierre from the Mississippi party). It was thirty feet long, and, when loaded to the gunwale, drew two feet of water. It had a deck twenty feet of its length forward, forming a cuddy-cabin, with a strong door, and of sufficient dimensions to contain our whole party with close crowding, as the boat was very broad. This part of it was bullet-proof, being wadded with oakum between two coatings of oak-plank; and in several positions we had small holes bored, through which we could fire upon an enemy in case of attack, as well as observe their movements; these holes, at the same time, gave us air and light, when we closed the door; and we had secure plugs to fit them when necessary. The remaining ten feet of the length was open, and here we could use as many as six oars; but our main dependence was upon poles which we employed by walking along the deck. We had also a short mast, easily shipped and unshipped, which was stepped about seven feet from the bow, and upon which we set a large square sail when the wind was fair, taking in mast and all when it was ahead.

In a division made in the bow, under the deck, we deposited ten kegs of good powder, and as much lead as we considered propor-tionate, one tenth ready moulded in rifle bullets. We had also stowed away here a small brass cannon and carriage, dismounted and taken to pieces, so as to lie in little compass, thinking that such a means of defence might possibly come into play at some period of our expedition. This cannon was one of three which

but short in stature, not being more than five feet three or four inches high; strongly built, with legs somewhat bowed. His physiognomy was of a Jewish cast, his lips thin, and his complexion saturnine.''

had been brought down the Missouri by the Spaniards two years previously, and lost overboard from a piroque, some miles above Petite Côte. A sand bar had so far altered the channel at the place where the canoe capsized that an Indian discovered one of the guns, and procured assistance to carry it down to the settlement, where he sold it for a gallon of whiskey. The people at Petite Côte then went up and procured the other two. They were very small guns, but of good metal and beautiful workmanship, being carved and ornamented with serpents like some of the French fieldpieces. Fifty iron balls were found with the guns, and these we procured. I mention the way in which we obtained this cannon, because it performed an important part in some of our operations, as will be found hereafter. Besides it, we had fifteen spare rifles, boxed up, and deposited forward with the other heavy goods. We put the weight here, to sink our bows well in the water, which is the best method, on account of the snags and sawyers in the river.

In the way of other arms we were sufficiently provided; each man having a stout hatchet and knife, besides his ordinary rifle and ammunition. Each boat was provided with a camp kettle, three large axes, a towing line, two oilcloths to cover the goods when necessary, and two large sponges for bailing. The piroque had also a small mast and sail (which I omitted to mention), and carried a quantity of gum, birchbark and watape, to make repairs with. She also had in charge all the Indian goods which we had thought necessary to bring with us, and which we purchased from the Mississippi boat. It was not our design to trade with the Indians; but these goods were offered us at a low rate, and we thought it better to take them, as they might prove of service. They consisted of silk and cotton handkerchiefs; thread, lines, and twine; hats, shoes, and hose; small cutlery and ironmongery; calicoes and printed cottons; Manchester goods; twist and carrot tobacco; milled blankets; and glass toys, beads, etc., etc. All these were done up in small packages, three of which were a man's load. The provisions were also put up so as to be easily handled; and a part was deposited in each boat. We had, altogether, two hundredweight of pork, six hundredweight of biscuit, and six hundredweight of pemmican. This we had made at Petite Côte, by the Canadians, who told us that it is used by the Northwest Fur Company in all their long voyages, when it is feared that game may not prove abundant. It is manufactured in a singular manner. The lean parts of the flesh of the larger animals is cut into thin slices, and placed on a wooden grate over a slow fire, or exposed to the sun (as ours was), or sometimes to the frost. When it is sufficiently dried in this way, it is pounded between two heavy stones, and will then keep for years. If, however, much of it is kept together, it ferments upon the breaking up of the frost in the spring and, if not well exposed to the air, soon decays. The inside fat, with that of the rump, is melted down and mixed, in a boiling state, with the pounded meat, half and half; it is then squeezed into bags, and is ready to eat without any further cooking, being very palatable without salt or vegetables. The best pemmican is made with the addition of marrow and dried berries, and is a capital article of food.* Our whiskey was in carboys, of five gallons each, and we had twenty of these, a hundred gallons in all.

When everything was well on board, with our whole company, including Thornton's dog, we found that there was but little room to spare, except in the big cabin, which we wished to preserve free of goods, as a sleeping place in bad weather; we had nothing in here except arms and ammunition, with some beaver traps and a carpet of bearskins. Our crowded state suggested an expedient which ought to have been adopted at all events: that of detaching four hunters from the party, to course along the river banks, and

*The pemmican here described by Mr Rodman is altogether new to us, and is very different from that with which our readers have no doubt been familiarized in the journals of Parry, Ross, Back, and other Northern voyagers. This, if we remember, was prepared by long continued boiling of the lean meat (carefully excluding fat) until the soup was reduced to a very small proportion of its original bulk, and assumed a pulpy consistency. To this residue, many spices and much salt were added, and great nutriment was supposed to be contained in the little bulk. The positive experience of an American surgeon, however, who had an opportunity of witnessing, and experimenting upon, the digestive process through an open wound in the stomach of a patient, has demonstrated that *bulk* is, in itself, an essential in this process, and that consequently the condensation of the nutritive property of food involves, in a great measure, a paradox.

keep us in game, as well as to act in capacity of scouts, to warn us of the approach of Indians. With this object we procured two good horses, giving one of them in charge of Robert and Meredith Greely, who were to keep upon the south bank; and the other in charge of Frank and Poindexter Greely, who were to course along the north side. By means of the horses they could bring in what game was shot.

This arrangement relieved our boats very considerably, lessening our number to eleven. In the small boat were two of the men from Petite Côte, with Toby and Pierre Junôt. In the large one were the Prophet (as we called him), or Alexander Wormley, John Greely, Andrew Thornton, three of the Petite Côte men, and myself, with Thornton's dog.

Our mode of proceeding was sometimes with oars, but not generally; we most frequently pulled ourselves along by the limbs of trees on shore; or, where the ground permitted it, we used a tow-line, which is the easiest way, some of us being on shore to haul, while some remained on board, to set the boat off shore with poles. Very often we poled together. In this method (which is a good one when the bottom is not too muddy, or full of quicksands, and when the depth of water is not too great) the Canadians are very expert, as well as at rowing. They use long, stiff and light poles, pointed with iron; with these they proceed to the bow of the boat, an equal number of men at each side; the face is then turned to the stern, and the pole inserted in the river, reaching the bottom; a firm hold being thus taken, the boatmen apply the heads of the poles to the shoulder, which is protected by a cushion, and, pushing in this manner, while they walk along the gunwale, the boat is urged forward with great force. There is no necessity for any steersman, while using the pole; for the poles direct the vessel with wonderful accuracy.

In these various modes of getting along, now and then varied with the necessity of wading, and dragging our vessels by hand, in rapid currents or through shallow water, we commenced our eventful voyage up the Missouri River. The skins, which were considered as the leading objects of the expedition, were to be obtained, principally, by hunting and trapping, as privately as possible, and without direct trade with the Indians, whom we had long learned to know as in the main a treacherous race, not to be dealt with safely in so small a party as ours. The furs usually collected by previous adventurers upon our contemplated route included beaver, otter, marten, lynx, mink, musquash, bear, fox, kitt-fox, wolverine, raccoon, fisher, wolf, buffalo, deer, and elk; but we proposed to confine ourselves to the more costly kinds.

The morning on which we set out from Petite Côte was one of the most inspiring and delicious; and nothing could exceed the hilarity of our whole party. The summer had hardly yet commenced, and the wind, which blew a strong breeze against us at first starting, had all the voluptuous softness of spring. The sun shone clearly, but with no great heat. The ice had disappeared from the river, and the current, which was pretty full, concealed all those marshy and ragged alluvia which disfigure the borders of the Missouri at low water. It had now the most majestic appearance, washing up among the willows and cottonwood on one side, and rushing, with a bold volume, by the sharp cliffs on the other. As I looked up the stream (which here stretched away to the westward, until the waters apparently met the sky in the great distance) and reflected on the immensity of territory through which those waters had probably passed, a territory as yet altogether unknown to white people, and perhaps abounding in the magnificent works of God, I felt an excitement of soul such as I had never before experienced, and secretly resolved that it should be no slight obstacle which should prevent my pushing up this noble river farther than any previous adventurer had done. At that moment I seemed possessed of an energy more than human, and my animal spirits rose to so high a degree that I could with difficulty content myself in the narrow limits of the boat. I longed to be with the Greelys on the bank, that I might give full vent to the feelings which inspired me, by leaping and running on the prairie. In these feelings Thornton participated strongly, evincing a deep interest in our expedition, and an admiration of the beautiful scenery around us, which rendered him from that moment a particular favourite with myself. I never, at any period of my life, felt so keenly as I then did, the want of some friend to whom I could converse freely and without danger of being misunderstood. The sudden loss of all my relatives by death had saddened, but not depressed, my spirits, which appeared to seek relief in a contemplation of the wild scenes of nature; and these scenes, and the reflections which they encouraged, could not, I found, be thoroughly enjoyed, without the society of some one person of reciprocal sentiments. Thornton was precisely the kind of individual to whom I could unburden my full heart, and unburden it of all its extravagant emotion, without fear of incurring a shadow of ridicule, and even in the certainty of finding a listener as impassioned as myself. I never, before or since, met with any one who so fully entered into my own notions respecting natural scenery; and this circumstance alone was sufficient to bind him to me in a firm friendship. We were as intimate, during our whole expedition, as brothers could possibly be, and I took no steps without consulting him. Pierre and myself were also friends, but there was not the tie of reciprocal thought between us, that strongest of all mortal bonds. His nature, although sensitive, was too volatile to comprehend all the devotional fervour of my own.

The incidents of the first day of our voyage had nothing remarkable in them; except that we had some difficulty in forcing our way, towards nightfall, by the mouth of a large cave on the south side of the river. This cave had a very dismal appearance as we passed it, being situated at the foot of a lofty bluff, full two hundred feet high, and jutting somewhat over the stream. We could not distinctly perceive the depth of the cavern, but it was about sixteen or seventeen feet high, and at least fifty in width.*

*The cave here mentioned is that called the "Tavern" by the traders and boatmen. Some grotesque images are painted on the cliffs, and commanded, at one period, great respect from the Indians. In speaking of this cavern, Captain Lewis says that it is 120 feet wide, 20 feet high, and 40 deep, and that the bluffs overhanging it are nearly 300 feet high. We wish to call attention to the circumstance that, in every point, Mr Rodman's account falls short of Captain Lewis's. With all his evident enthusiasm, our traveller is never prone to the exaggeration of facts. In a great variety of instances like the present, it will be found that his statements respecting quantity (in the full sense of the term) always fall within the truth, as this truth is since ascertained. We regard this as a remarkable trait in his

The current ran past it with great velocity and, as from the nature of the cliff we could now tow, it required the utmost exertion to make our way by it; which we at length effected by getting all of us, with the exception of one man, into the large boat. This one remained in the piroque, and anchored it below the cave. By uniting our force, then, in rowing, we brought the large boat up beyond the difficult pass, paying out a line to the piroque as we proceeded, and by this line hauling it up after us, when we had fairly ascended. We passed, during the day, Bonhomme, and Osage Femme rivers, with two small creeks and several islands of little extent. We made about twenty-five miles, notwithstanding the head wind, and encamped at night on the north bank, and at the foot of a rapid called Diable.

June 4. Early this morning, Frank and Poindexter Greely came into our camp with a fat buck, upon which we all breakfasted in high glee, and afterwards pushed on with spirit. At the Diable rapid, the current sets with much force against some rocks which jut out from the south, and render the navigation difficult. A short distance above this we met with several quicksand bars, which put us to trouble; the banks of the river here fall in continually, and, in the process of time, must greatly alter the bed. At eight o'clock we had a fine fresh wind from the eastward, and, with its assistance, made rapid progress, so that by night we had gone perhaps thirty miles, or more. We passed, on the north, the river Du Bois, a creek called Charité,* and several small islands. The river was rising fast as we came to, at night, under a group of cottonwood trees, there being no ground near at hand upon

mind; and it is assuredly one which would entitle his observations to the highest credit, when they concern regions about which we know nothing beyond these observations. In all points which relate to effects, on the contrary, Mr Rodman's peculiar temperament leads him into excess. For example, he speaks of the cavern now in question as of a "dismal appearance", and the colouring of his narrative respecting it is derived principally from the sombre hue of his own spirit, at the time of passing the rock. It will be as well to bear these distinctions in mind, as we read his Journal. His facts are never heightened; his impressions from these facts must have, to ordinary perceptions, a tone of exaggeration. Yet there is no falsity in this exaggeration, except in view of a general sentiment upon the thing seen and described. As regards his own mind, the apparent gaudiness of colour is the absolute and only true tint.

*La Charette? Du Bois is no doubt Wood River.

which we were disposed to encamp. It was beautiful weather, and I felt too much excited to sleep; so, asking Thornton to accompany me, I took a stroll into the country, and did not return until nearly daylight. The rest of our crew occupied the cabin, for the first time, and found it quite roomy enough for five or six more persons. They had been disturbed, in the night, by a strange noise overhead, on deck, the origin of which they had not been able to ascertain; as, when some of the party rushed out to see, the disturber had disappeared. From the account given of the noise, I concluded that it must have proceeded from an Indian dog, who had scented our fresh provisions (the buck of yesterday) and was endeavouring to make off with a portion. In this view I felt perfectly satisfied; but the occurrence suggested the great risk we ran in not posting a regular watch at night, and it was agreed to do so for the future.

[Having thus given, in Mr Rodman's own words, the incidents of the two first days of the voyage, we forbear to follow him minutely in his passage up the Missouri to the mouth of the Platte, at which he arrived on the 10th of August. The character of the river throughout this extent is so well known, and has been so frequently described, that any further account of it is unnecessary; and the Journal takes note of little else, at this portion of the tour, than the natural features of the country, together with the ordinary boating and hunting occurrences. The party made three several halts for the purpose of trapping, but met with no great success; and finally concluded to push farther into the heart of the country, before making any regular attempts at collecting peltries. Only two events of moment are recorded, for the two months which we omit. One of these was the death of a Canadian, Jacques Lauzanne, by the bite of a rattlesnake; the other was the encountering of a Spanish commission sent to intercept and turn the party back, by order of the commandant of the province. The officer in charge of the detachment, however, was so much interested in the expedition, and took so great a fancy to Mr Rodman, that our travellers were permitted to proceed. Many small bodies of Osage and Kanzas Indians hovered occasionally about the boats, but evinced nothing of hostility. We leave the voyagers for the present, therefore, at the mouth of the river Platte, on the 10th of August 1791, their number having been reduced to fourteen.]

II

[HAVING REACHED the mouth of the river Platte, our voyagers encamped for three days, during which they were busily occupied in drying and airing their goods and provisions, making new oars and poles, and repairing the birch canoe, which had sustained material injury. The hunters brought in an abundance of game, with which the boats were loaded to repletion. Deer was had for the asking, and turkeys and fat grouse were met with in great plenty. The party, moreover, regaled on several species of fish, and, at a short distance from the river banks, found an exquisite kind of wild grape. No Indians had been seen for better than a fortnight, as this was the hunting season, and they were doubtless engaged in the prairies, taking buffalo. After perfectly recruiting, the voyagers broke up their encampment, and pushed on up the Missouri. We resume the words of the Journal.]

August 14.   We started with a delightful breeze from the S.E., and kept along by the southern shore, taking advantage of the eddy, and going at a great rate, notwithstanding the current, which, in the middle, was unusually full and strong. At noon, we stopped to examine some remarkable mounds on the south-western shore, at a spot where the ground seems to have sunk considerably to an extent of three hundred acres or more. A large pond is in the vicinity, and appears to have drained the low tract. This is covered with mounds of various sizes and shapes, all formed of sand and mud, the highest being nearest the river. I could not make up my mind whether these hillocks were of natural or artificial construction. I should have supposed them made by the Indians, but for the general appearance of the soil, which had apparently been subjected to the violent action of water.* We stayed at this spot the rest of the day, having made altogether twenty miles.

August 15.   Today we had a heavy, disagreeable head wind, and made only fifteen miles, with great labour; encamping at night beneath a bluff on the north shore, this being the first bluff on that side which we had seen since leaving the Nodaway River. In the night it came on to rain in torrents, and the Greelÿs brought in their horses, and ensconced themselves in the cabin. Robert swam the river with his horse from the south shore, and then took the canoe across for Meredith. He appeared to think nothing of either of these feats, although the night was one of the darkest and most boisterous I ever saw, and the river was much swollen. We all sat in the cabin very comfortably, for the weather was quite cool, and were kept awake for a long time by the anecdotes of Thornton, who told story after story of his adventures with the Indians on the Mississippi. His huge dog appeared to listen with profound attention to every word that was said. Whenever any particularly incredible circumstance was related, Thornton would gravely refer to him as a witness. "Nep," he would say, "don't you remember that time?" or "Nep can swear to the truth of that —can't you, Nep?" when the animal would roll up his eyes immediately, loll out his monstrous tongue, and wag his great head up and down, as much as to say: "Oh, it's every bit as true as the Bible." Although we all knew that this trick had been taught the dog, yet for our lives we could not forbear shouting with laughter, whenever Thornton would appeal to him.

August 16.   Early this morning passed an island, and a creek about fifteen yards wide, and, at a farther distance of twelve miles, a large island in the middle of the river. We had now, generally, high prairie and timbered hills on the north, with low ground on the south, covered with cottonwood. The river was excessively crooked, but not so rapid as before we passed the

---

*These mounds are now well understood to indicate the position of the ancient village of the Ottoes, who were once a very powerful tribe. Being reduced by continual hostilities, they sought protection of the Pawnees, and migrated to the south of the Platte, about thirty miles from its mouth.

Platte. Altogether there is less timber than formerly; what there is, is mostly elm, cottonwood, hickory, and walnut, with some oak. Had a strong wind nearly all day, and by means of the eddy and this, we made twenty-five miles before night. Our encampment was on the south, upon a large plain, covered with high grass, and bearing a great number of plum trees and currant bushes. In our rear was a steep woody ridge, ascending which we found another prairie extending back for about a mile, and stopped again by a similar woody ridge, followed by another vast prairie, going off into the distance as far as the eye can reach. From the cliffs just above us we had one of the most beautiful prospects in the world.*

August 17. We remained at the encampment all day, and occupied ourselves in various employments. Getting Thornton, with his dog, to accompany me, I strolled to some distance to the southward, and was enchanted with the voluptuous beauty of the country. The prairies exceeded in beauty anything told in the tales of the *Arabian Nights.* On the edges of the creeks there was a wild mass of flowers which looked more like art than nature, so profusely and fantastically were their vivid colours blended together. Their rich odour was almost oppressive. Every now and then we came to a kind of green island of trees, placed amid an ocean of purple, blue, orange and crimson blossoms, all waving to and fro in the wind. These islands consisted of the most majestic forest oaks, and, beneath them, the grass resembled a robe of the softest green velvet, while up their huge stems there clambered generally a profusion of grapevines, laden with delicious ripe fruit. The Missouri in the distance presented the most majestic appearance; and many of the real islands with which it was studded were entirely covered with plum bushes, or other shrubbery, except where crossed in various directions by narrow, mazy paths, like the alleys in an English flower-garden; and in these alleys we could always see either elks or antelopes, who had no doubt made them. We returned, at sunset, to the

*The Council Bluffs.

encampment, delighted with our excursion. The night was warm, and we were excessively annoyed by mosquitoes.

August 18.   Today passed through a narrow part of the river, not more than two hundred yards wide, with a rapid channel, much obstructed with logs and driftwood. Ran the large boat on a sawyer, and half filled her with water before we could extricate her from the difficulty. We were obliged to halt, in consequence, and overhaul our things. Some of the biscuit was injured, but none of the powder. Remained all day, having only made five miles.

August 19.   We started early this morning and made great headway. The weather was cool and cloudy, and at noon we had a drenching shower. Passed a creek on the south, the mouth of which is nearly concealed by a large sand island of singular appearance. Went about fifteen miles beyond this. The highlands now recede from the river, and are probably from ten to twenty miles apart. On the north is a good deal of fine timber, but on the south very little. Near the river are beautiful prairies, and along the banks we procured four or five different species of grape, all of good flavour and quite ripe; one is a large purple grape of excellent quality. The hunters came into camp at night from both sides of the river, and brought us more game than we well knew what to do with—grouse, turkeys, two deer, an antelope and a quantity of yellow birds with black striped wings; these latter proved delicious eating. We made about twenty miles during the day.

August 20.   The river, this morning, was full of sand bars and other obstructions; but we proceeded with spirit, and reached the mouth of a pretty large creek, before night, at a distance of twenty miles from our last encampment. The creek comes in from the north, and has a large island opposite its mouth. Here we made our camp, with the resolution of remaining four or five days to trap beaver, as we saw great signs of them in the neighbourhood. This island was one of the most fairy-looking situations in the world, and filled my mind with the most delightful and novel emotions. The whole scenery rather resembled what I had dreamed of when a boy than an actual reality. The banks sloped down very gradually into the water, and were carpeted with a soft grass of a brilliant green hue, which was visible under the surface of the stream for some distance from the shore; especially on the north side, where the clear creek fell into the river. All round the island, which was probably about twenty acres in extent, was a complete fringe of cottonwood, the trunks loaded with grape-vines in full fruit, and so closely interlocking with each other that we could scarcely get a glimpse of the river between the leaves. Within this circle the grass was somewhat higher, and of a coarser texture, with a pale yellow or white streak down the middle of each blade, and giving out a remarkably delicious perfume, resem-bling that of the vanilla bean, but much stronger, so that the whole atmosphere was loaded with it. The common English sweet grass is no doubt of the same genus, but greatly inferior in beauty and fragrance. Interspersed among it in every direction, were myriads of the most brilliant flowers, in full bloom, and most of them of fine odour—blue, pure white, bright yellow, purple, crimson, gaudy scarlet, and some with streaked leaves like tulips. Little knots of cherry trees and plum bushes grew in various directions about, and there were many narrow winding paths which circled the island, and which had been made by elks or antelopes. Nearly in the centre was a spring of sweet and clear water, which bubbled up from among a cluster of steep rocks, covered from head to foot with moss and flowering vines. The whole bore a wonderful resem-blance to an artificial flower-garden, but was infinitely more beautiful, looking rather like some of those scenes of enchant-ment which we read of in old books. We were all in ecstasy with the spot, and prepared our camp in the highest glee, amid its wilderness of sweets.

[The party remained here a week, during which time, the neigh-bouring country to the north was explored in many directions, and some peltries obtained, especially upon the creek mentioned. The weather was fine, and the enjoyment of the voyagers suffered no alloy, in their terrestrial Paradise. Mr Rodman, however, omitted no necessary precautions, and sentries were regularly posted every night, when all hands assembled at camp, and made merry. Such feasting and drinking were never before known, the Canadians proving themselves the very best fellows in the world at a song or over a flagon. They did nothing but eat, and cook, and dance, and shout French carols at the top of their voice. During the day they were chiefly entrusted with the charge of the encampment, while the steadier members of the party were absent upon hunting or trapping expeditions. In one of these Mr Rodman enjoyed an excellent opportunity of observing the habits of the beaver; and his account of this singular animal is highly interesting; the more so as it differs materially, in some points, from the ordinary descriptions.

He was attended, as usual, by Thornton and his dog, and had traced up a small creek to its source in the highlands about ten miles from the river. The party came at length to a place where a large swamp had been made by the beavers, in damming up the creek. A thick grove of willows occupied one extremity of the swamp, some of them overhanging the water at a spot where several of the animals were observed. Our adventurers crept stealthily round to these willows, and, making Neptune lie down at a little distance, succeeded in climbing, unobserved, into a large and thick tree, where they could look immediately down upon all that was going on.

The beavers were repairing a portion of their dam, and every step of their progress was distinctly seen. One by one the architects were perceived to approach the edge of the swamp, each with a small branch in his mouth. With this he proceeded to the dam, and placed it carefully, and longitudinally, on the part which had given way. Having done this, he dived immediately, and in a few seconds reappeared above the surface with a quantity of stiff mud, which he first squeezed so as to drain it of its moisture in a great degree, and then applied with his feet and tail (using the latter as a trowel) to the branch which he had just laid upon the breach. He then made off among the trees, and was quickly succeeded by another of the community, who went through precisely the same operation.

In this way the damage sustained by the dam was in a fair way of being soon repaired. Messieurs Rodman and Thornton observed the progress of the work for more than two hours, and bear testimony to the exquisite skill of the artisans. But as soon as a beaver left the edge of the swamp in search of a branch, he was lost sight of among the willows, much to the chagrin of the observers, who were anxious to watch his further operations. By clambering a little higher up in the tree, however, they discovered everything. A small sycamore had been felled, apparently, and was now nearly denuded of all its fine branches, a few beavers still nibbling off some that remained, and proceeding with them to the dam. In the meantime a great number of the animals surrounded a much older and larger tree, which they were busily occupied in cutting down. There were as many as fifty or sixty of the creatures around the trunk, of which number six or seven would work at once, leaving off one by one, as each became weary, a fresh one stepping into the vacated place. When our travellers first observed the sycamore, it had been already cut through to a great extent, but only on the side nearest the swamp, upon the edge of which it grew. The incision was nearly a foot wide, and as cleanly made as if done with an axe; and the ground at the bottom of the tree was covered with fine longitudinal slips, like straws, which had been nibbled out, and not eaten; as it appears that these animals only use the bark for food. When at work some sat upon the hind legs, in the posture so common with squirrels, and gnawed at the wood, their forefeet resting upon the edge of the cut, and their heads thrust far into the aperture. Two of them, however, were entirely within the incision; lying at length, and working with great eagerness for a short time, when they were relieved by their companions.

Although the position of our voyagers was anything but comfortable, so great was their curiosity to witness the felling of the sycamore that they resolutely maintained their post until sunset, an interval of eight hours from the time of ascending. Their chief embarrassment was on Neptune's account, who could with difficulty be kept from plunging into the swamp after the plasterers who were repairing the dam. The noise he made had several times disturbed the nibblers at the tree, who would every now and then start, as if all actuated by one mind, and listen attentively for many minutes. As evening approached, however, the dog gave over his freaks, and lay quiet; while the beavers went on uninterruptedly with their labour.

Just as the sun began to set, a sudden commotion was observed among the woodcutters, who all started from the tree, and flew round to the side which was untouched. In an instant afterwards it was seen to settle down gradually on the gnawed side, till the lips of the incision met; but still it did not fall, being sustained partially by the unsundered bark. This was now attacked with zeal by as many nibblers as could find room to work at it, and very quickly severed; when the huge tree, to which the proper inclination had already been so ingeniously given, fell with a tremendous crash, and spread a great portion of its topmost branches over the surface of the swamp. This matter accomplished, the whole community seemed to think a holiday was deserved and, ceasing work at once, began to chase each other about in the water, diving, and slapping the surface with their tails.

The account here given of the method employed by the beaver in its woodcutting operations is more circumstantial than any we have yet seen, and seems to be conclusive in regard to the question of design on the animal's part. The intention of making the tree fall towards the water appears here to be obvious. Captain Bonneville, it will be remembered, discredits the alleged sagacity of the animal in this respect, and thinks it has no further aim than to get the tree down, without any subtle calculation in respect to its mode of descent. This attribute, he thinks, has been ascribed to it from the circumstance that trees in general, which grow near the margin of water, either lean bodily towards the stream, or stretch their most ponderous limbs in that direction, in search of the light, space and air which are there usually found. The beaver, he says, attacks, of course, those trees which are nearest at hand, and on the banks of the stream or pond, and these, when cut through, naturally preponderate towards the water. This suggestion is well-timed, but by no means conclusive against the design of the beaver whose sagacity, at best, is far beneath that which is positively ascertained in respect to many classes of inferior animals, infinitely below that of the lion-ant, of the bee, and of the coralliferi. The probability is that, were two trees offered to the choice of the beaver, one of which preponderated to the water, and the other did not, he would, in felling the first, omit, as unnecessary, the precautions just described, but observe them in felling the second.

In a subsequent portion of the Journal other particulars are given respecting the habits of the singular animal in question, and of the mode of trapping it employed by the party, and we give them here for the sake of continuity. The principal food of the beavers is bark, and of this they put by regularly a large store for winter provision, selecting the proper kind with care and deliberation. A whole tribe, consisting sometimes of two or three hundred, will set out together upon a foraging expedition, and pass through groves of trees all apparently similar, until a particular one suits their fancy. This they cut down, and, breaking off its most tender branches, divide them into short slips of equal length, and divest these slips of their bark, which they carry to the nearest stream leading to their village, thence floating it home. Occasionally the slips are stored away for the winter without being stripped of the bark; and, in this event, they are careful to remove the refuse wood from their dwellings, as soon as they have eaten the rind, taking the sticks to some distance. During the spring of the year the males are never found with the tribe at home, but always by themselves, either singly, or in parties of two or three, when they appear to lose their usual habits of sagacity, and fall an easy prey to the arts of the trapper. In summer they return home, and busy themselves, with the females, in making provision for winter. They are described as exceedingly ferocious animals when irritated.

Now and then they may be caught upon shore; especially the males in spring, who are then fond of roving to some distance from the water in search of food. When thus caught, they are easily killed with a blow from a stick; but the most certain and efficacious mode of taking them is by means of the trap. This is simply constructed to catch the foot of the animal. The trapper places it usually in some position near the shore, and just below the surface of the water, fastening it by a small chain to a pole stuck in the mud. In the mouth of the machine is placed one end of a small branch, the other end rising above the surface, and well soaked in the liquid bait whose odour is found to be attractive to the beaver. As soon as the animal scents it, he rubs his nose against the twig, and in so doing steps upon the trap, springs it, and is caught. The trap is made very light, for the convenience of portage, and the prey would easily swim off with it but for its being fastened to the pole by a chain; no other species of fastening could resist his teeth. The experienced trapper readily detects the presence of beaver in any pond or stream, discovering them by a thousand appearances which would afford no indication to the unpractised observer.

Many of the identical woodcutters whom the two *voyageurs* had watched so narrowly from the treetop fell afterwards a victim to trap, and their fine furs became a prey to the spoilers, who made sad havoc in the lodge at the swamp. Other waters in the neighbourhood also afforded the travellers much sport; and they long remembered the island at the creek's mouth, by the name of Beaver Island, in consequence. They left this little paradise in high spirits on the twenty-seventh of the month and, pursuing their hitherto somewhat uneventful voyage up the river, arrived, by the first of September, without any incident of note, at the mouth of a large river on the south, to which they gave the name of Currant River, from some berries abounding upon its margin, but which was, beyond doubt, the Quicourre. The principal objects of which the Journal takes notice in this interval are the numerous herds of buffalo which darkened the prairies in every direction, and the remains of a fortification on the south shore of the river, nearly opposite the upper extremity of what has been since called Bonhomme Island. Of these remains a minute description is given, which tallies in every important particular with that of Captains Lewis and Clarke. The travellers had passed the Little Sioux, Floyd's, the Great Sioux, White Stone and Jacques rivers on the north; with Wawandysenche Creek and White Paint River on the south, but at neither of these streams did they stop to trap for any long period. They had also passed the great village of the Omahas, of which the Journal takes no notice whatever. This village, at the time, consisted of full three hundred houses, and was inhabited by a numerous and powerful tribe; but it is not immediately upon the banks of the Missouri, and the boats probably went by it during the night, for the party had begun to adopt this mode of progress, through fear of the Sioux. We resume the narrative of Mr Rodman, with the second of September.]

September 2. We had now reached a part of the river where, according to all report, a great deal of danger was to be apprehended from the Indians, and we became extremely cautious in our movements. This was the region inhabited by the Sioux, a warlike and ferocious tribe, who had, upon several occasions, evinced hostility to the whites, and were known to be constantly at war with all the neighbouring tribes. The Canadians had many incidents to relate respecting their savage propensities, and I had much apprehension lest those cowardly creatures should take an opportunity of deserting, and retracing their way to the Mississippi. To lessen the chances of this, I removed one of them from the piroque, and supplied his place by Poindexter Greely. All the Greelys came in from the shore, turning loose the horses. Our arrangement was now as follows: in the piroque, Poindexter Greely, Pierre Junôt, Toby, and one Canadian; in the large boat, myself, Thornton, Wormley; John, Frank, Robert, and Meredith Greely; and three Canadians, with the dog. We set sail about dusk, and, having a brisk wind from the south, made good headway, although as night came on we were greatly embarrassed by the shoals. We continued our course without interruption, however, until a short time before daybreak, when we ran into the mouth of a creek, and concealed the boats among the underwood.

September 3 and 4. During both of these days it rained and blew with excessive violence, so that we did not leave our retreat at all. The weather depressed our spirits very much, and the narratives of the Canadians about the terrible Sioux did not serve to raise them. We all congregated in the cabin of the large boat, and held a council in regard to our future movements. The Greelys were for a bold push through the dangerous country, maintaining that the stories of the *voyageurs* were mere exaggerations, and that the Sioux would only be a little troublesome, without proceeding to hostility. Wormley and Thornton, however, as well as Pierre (all of whom had much experience in the Indian character) thought that our present policy was the best, although it would necessarily detain us much longer on our voyage than would otherwise be the case. My own opinion coincided with theirs; in our present course we might escape any collision with the Sioux, and I did not regard the delay as a matter of consequence.

September 5. We set off at night, and proceeded for about ten miles, when the day began to appear, and we hid the boats as before, in a narrow creek, which was well adapted to the purpose, as its mouth was almost blocked up by a thickly-wooded island. It again came on to rain furiously, and we were all drenched to the skin before we could arrange matters for turning in, in the cabin. Our spirits were much depressed by the bad weather, and the Canadians especially were in a miserable state of dejection. We had now come to a narrow part of the river where the current was strong, and the cliffs on both sides overhung the water, and were thickly wooded with lynn, oak, black walnut, ash, and chestnut. Through such a gorge we knew it would be exceedingly difficult to pass without observation, even at night, and our apprehensions of attack were greatly increased. We resolved not to recommence our journey until late, and then to proceed with the most stealthy caution. In the meantime we posted a sentry on shore and one in the piroque, while the rest of us busied ourselves in overhauling the arms and ammunition, and preparing for the worst.

About ten o'clock we were getting ready to start, when the dog gave a low growl, which made us all fly to our rifles; but the cause of the disturbance proved to be a single Indian of the Ponca tribe, who came up frankly to our sentry on shore, and extended his hand. We brought him on board, and gave him whiskey, when he became very communicative, and told us that his tribe, who lived some miles lower down the river, had been watching our movements for several days past, but that the Poncas were friends and would not molest the whites, and would trade with us upon our return. They had sent him now to caution the whites against the Sioux, who were great robbers, and who were lying in wait for the party at a bend in the river, twenty miles farther up. There were three bands of them, he said, and it was their intention to kill us all, in revenge for an insult sustained by one of their chiefs, many years previously, at the hands of a French trapper.

III

[WE LEFT OUR travellers, on the fifth of September, apprehending a present attack from the Sioux. Exaggerated accounts of the ferocity of this tribe had inspired the party with an earnest wish to avoid them; but the tale told by the friendly Ponca made it evident that a collision must take place. The night voyages were therefore abandoned as impolitic, and it was resolved to put a bold face upon the matter, and try what could be effected by blustering. The remainder of the night of the fifth was spent in warlike demonstration. The large boat was cleared for action as well as possible, and the fiercest aspect assumed which the nature of the case would permit. Among other preparations for defence, the cannon was got out from below, and placed forward upon the cuddy deck, with a load of bullets, by way of canister shot. Just before sunrise the adventurers started up the river in high bravado, aided by a heavy wind. That the enemy might perceive no semblance of fear or mistrust, the whole party joined the Canadians in an uproarious boat song at the top of their voices, making the woods reverberate, and the buffaloes stare.

The Sioux, indeed, appear to have been Mr Rodman's bugbears *par excellence,* and he dwells upon them and their exploits with peculiar emphasis. The narrative embodies a detailed account of the tribe, an account which we can only follow in such portions as appear to possess novelty, or other important interest. "Sioux" is the French term for the Indians in question; the English have corrupted it into "Sues". Their primitive name is said to be "Darcotas". Their original seats were on the Mississippi, but they had gradually extended their dominions, and, at the date of the Journal, occupied almost the whole of that vast territory circumscribed by the Mississippi, the Saskatchawine, the Missouri, and the Red River of Lake Winnipeg. They were subdivided into numerous clans. The Darcotas proper were the Winowacants, called the Gens du Lac by the French, consisting of about five hundred warriors, and living on both sides of the Mississippi, in the vicinity of the Falls of St Anthony. Neighbours of the Winowacants, and residing north of them on the river St Peter's, were the Wappatomies, about two hundred men. Still farther up the St Peter's lived a band of one hundred, called the Wappytooties, among themselves, and by the French the Gens des Feuilles. Higher up the river yet, and near its source, resided the Sissytoonies, in number two hundred or thereabouts. On the Missouri dwelt the Yanktons and the Tetons. Of the first tribe there were two branches, the northern and southern, of which the former led an Arab life in the plains at the sources of the Red, Sioux and Jacques rivers, being in number about five hundred. The southern branch kept possession of the tract lying between the river Des Moines on the one hand, and the rivers Jacques and Sioux on the other. But the Sioux most renowned for deeds of violence are the Tetons; and of these there were four tribes: the Saonies, the Minnakenozzies, the Okydandies, and the Bois-Brulés. These last, a body of whom were now lying in wait to intercept the *voyageurs,* were the most savage and formidable of the whole race, numbering about two hundred men, and residing on both sides of the Missouri near the rivers called by Captains Lewis and Clarke, the White and Teton. Just below the Chayenne River were the Okydandies, one hundred and fifty. The Minnakenozzies, two hundred and fifty, occupied a tract between the Chayenne and the Watarhoo; and the Saonies, the largest of the Teton bands, counting as many as three hundred warriors, were found in the vicinity of the Warreconne.

Besides these four divisions (the regular Sioux) there were five tribes of seceders called Assiniboins; the Menatopae Assiniboins, two hundred, on Mouse River, between the Assiniboin and the Missouri; the Gens de Feuilles Assiniboins, two hundred and fifty, occupying both sides of White River; the Big Devils, four hundred and fifty, wandering about the heads of Porcupine and Milk rivers; with two other bands whose names are not mentioned, but who roved on the Saskatchawine, and numbered together about seven hundred men. These seceders were often at war with the parent or original Sioux.

In person, the Sioux generally are an ugly, ill-made race, their limbs being much too small for the trunk, according to our ideas of the human form; their cheekbones are high, and their eyes protruding and dull. The heads of the men are shaved, with the exception of a small spot on the crown, whence a long tuft is permitted to fall in plaits upon the shoulders; this tuft is an object of scrupulous care, but is now and then cut off, upon an occasion of grief or solemnity. A full-dressed Sioux chief presents a striking appearance. The whole surface of the body is painted with grease and coal. A shirt of skins is worn as far down as the waist, while round the middle is a girdle of the same material, and sometimes of cloth, about an inch in width; this supports a piece of blanket or fur passing between the thighs. Over the shoulders is a white-dressed buffalo mantle, the hair of which is worn next the skin in fair weather, but turned outwards in wet. This robe is large enough to envelop the whole body, and is frequently ornamented with porcupine quills (which make a rattling noise as the warrior moves), as well as with a great variety of rudely painted figures, emblematical of the wearer's military character. Fastened to the top of the head is worn a hawk's feather, adorned with porcupine quills. Leggings of dressed antelope skin serve the purpose of pantaloons, and have seams at the sides about two inches wide, and bespotted here and there with small tufts of human hair, the trophies of some scalping excursion. The moccasins are of elk or buffalo skin, the hair worn inwards; on great occasions the chief is seen with the skin of a polecat dangling at the heel of each boot. The Sioux are indeed partial to this noisome animal, whose fur is in high favour for tobacco pouches and other appendages.

The dress of a chieftain's squaw is also remarkable. Her hair is suffered to grow long, is parted across the forehead, and hangs loosely behind, or is collected into a kind of net. Her moccasins do not differ from her husband's; but her leggings extend upwards only as far as the knee, where they are met by an awkward shirt of elk skin depending to the ankles, and supported above by a string going over the shoulders. This shirt is usually confined to the waist by a girdle, and over all is thrown a buffalo mantle like that of the men. The tents of the Teton Sioux are described as of neat construction, being formed of white-dressed buffalo hide, well secured and supported by poles.

The region infested by the tribe in question extends along the banks of the Missouri for some hundred and fifty miles or more, and is chiefly prairie land, but is occasionally diversified by hills. These latter are always deeply cut by gorges or ravines, which in the middle of summer are dry, but form the channels of muddy and impetuous torrents during the season of rain. Their edges are fringed with thick woods, as well at top as at bottom; but the prevalent aspect of the country is that of a bleak lowland, with rank herbage, and without trees. The soil is strongly impregnated with mineral substances in great variety; among others with glauber salts, copperas, sulphur and alum, which tinge the water of the river and impart to it a nauseous odour and taste. The wild animals most usual are the buffalo, deer, elk, and antelope. We again resume the words of the Journal.]

September 6. The country was open, and the day remarkably pleasant: so that we were all in pretty good spirits notwithstanding the expectation of attack. So far, we had not caught even a glimpse of an Indian, and we were making rapid way through their dreaded territory. I was too well aware, however, of the savage tactics to suppose that we were not narrowly watched, and had made up my mind that we should hear something of the Tetons at the first gorge which would afford them a convenient lurking-place.

About noon a Canadian bawled out, ''The Sioux! the Sioux!'' and directed attention to a long narrow ravine which intersected the prairie on our left, extending from the banks of the Missouri as far as the eye could reach, in a southwardly course. This gully was the bed of a creek, but its waters were now low, and the sides rose up like huge regular walls on each side. By the aid of a spyglass I perceived at once the cause of the alarm given by the *voyageur*. A large party of mounted savages were coming down the gorge in Indian file, with the evident intention of taking us unawares. Their calumet feathers had been the means of their detection; for every now and then we could see some of these bobbing up above the edge of the gully, as the bed of the ravine forced the wearer to rise higher than usual. We could tell that they were on horseback by the motion of these feathers. The party was coming upon us with great rapidity; and I gave the word to pull on with all haste so as to pass the mouth of the creek before they reached it. As soon as the Indians perceived by our increased speed that they were discovered, they immediately raised a yell, scrambled out of the gorge, and galloped down upon us, to the number of about one hundred.

Our situation was now somewhat alarming. At almost any other part of the Missouri which we had passed during the day, I should not have cared so much for these freebooters; but, just here, the banks were remarkably steep and high, partaking of the character of the creek banks, and the savages were enabled to overlook us completely, while the cannon, upon which we had placed so much reliance, could not be brought to bear upon them at all. What added to our difficulty was that the current in the middle of the river was so turbulent and strong that we could make no headway against it except by dropping arms, and employing our whole force at the oars. The water near the northern shore was too shallow even for the piroque, and our only mode of proceeding, if we designed to proceed at all, was by pushing in within a moderate stone's throw of the left or southern bank, where we were completely at the mercy of the Sioux, but where we could make good headway by means of our poles and the wind, aided by the eddy. Had the savages attacked us at this juncture I cannot see how we could have escaped them. They were all well provided with bows and arrows, and small round shields, presenting a very noble and picturesque appearance. Some of the chiefs had spears, with fanciful flags attached, and were really gallant-looking men.

Either good luck upon our own parts, or great stupidity on the parts of the Indians, relieved us very unexpectedly from the dilemma. The savages, having galloped up to the edge of the cliff just above us, set up another yell, and commenced a variety of gesticulations, whose meaning we at once knew to be that we should stop and come on shore. I had expected this demand, and had made up my mind that it would be most prudent to pay no attention to it at all, but proceed on our course. My refusal to stop had at least one good effect, for it appeared to mystify the Indians most wonderfully, who could not be brought to understand the measure in the least, and stared at us, as we kept on our way without answering them, in the most ludicrous amazement. Presently they commenced an agitated conversation among themselves, and at last finding that nothing could be made of us, fairly turned their horses' heads to the southward and galloped out of sight, leaving us as much surprised as rejoiced at their departure.

In the meantime we made the most of the opportunity, and pushed on with might and main, in order to get out of the region of steep banks before the anticipated return of our foes. In about two hours we again saw them in the south, at a great distance, and their number much augmented. They came on at full gallop, and were soon at the river; but our position was now much more advantageous, for the banks were sloping, and there were no trees to shelter the savages from our shot. The current, moreover, was not so rapid as before, and we were enabled to keep in mid-channel. The party, it seems, had only retreated to procure an interpreter, who now appeared upon a large grey horse, and, coming into the river as far as he could without swimming, called out to us in bad French to stop, and come on shore. To this I made one of the Canadians reply that, to oblige our friends the Sioux, we would willingly stop for a short time, and converse, but that it was inconvenient for us to come on shore, as we could not do so without incommoding our great Medicine (here the Canadian pointed to the cannon), who was anxious to proceed on his voyage, and whom we were afraid to disobey.

At this they began again their agitated whisperings and gesticulations among themselves, and seemed quite at a loss what to do. In the meantime the boats had been brought to anchor in a favourable position, and I was resolved to fight now, if necessary, and endeavour to give the freebooters so warm a reception as would inspire them with wholesome dread for the future. I reflected that it was nearly impossible to keep on good terms with these Sioux, who were our enemies at heart, and who could only be restrained from pillaging and murdering us by a conviction of our prowess. Should we comply with their present demands, go on shore, and even succeed in purchasing a temporary safety by concessions and donations, such conduct would not avail us in the end, and would be rather a palliation than a radical cure of the evil. They would be sure to glut their vengeance sooner or later, and, if they suffered us to go on our way now, might hereafter attack us at a disadvantage, when it might be as much as we could do to repel them, to say nothing of inspiring them with awe. Situated as we were here, it was in our power to give them a lesson they would be apt to remember; and we might never be in so good a situation again. Thinking thus, and all except the Canadians agreeing with me in opinion, I determined to assume a bold stand, and rather provoke hostilities than avoid them. This was our true policy. The savages had no firearms which we could discover, except an old carbine carried by one of the chiefs; and their arrows would not prove very effective weapons when employed at so great a distance as that now between us. In regard to their number, we did not care much for that. Their position was one which would expose them to the full sweep of our cannon.

When Jules (the Canadian) had finished his speech about
incommoding our great Medicine, and when the consequent
agitation had somewhat subsided among the savages, the interpreter spoke again and propounded three queries. He wished to
know, first, whether we had any tobacco, or whiskey, or fire-
guns; secondly, whether we did not wish the aid of the Sioux in
rowing our large boat up the Missouri as far as the country of the
Ricarees, who were great rascals; and, thirdly, whether our great
Medicine was not a very large and strong green grasshopper.

To these questions, propounded with profound gravity, Jules
replied, by my directions, as follows: first, that we had plenty of
whiskey, as well as tobacco, with an inexhaustible supply of fire-
guns and powder; but that our great Medicine had just told us that
the Tetons were greater rascals than the Ricarees; that they were
our enemies; that they had been lying in wait to intercept and kill
us for many days past; that we must give them nothing at all, and
hold no intercourse with them whatever; we should therefore be
afraid to give them anything, even if so disposed, for fear of the
anger of the great Medicine, who was not to be trifled with.
Secondly, that, after the character just given the Sioux Tetons, we
could not think of employing them to row our boat; and, thirdly,
that it was a good thing for them (the Sioux) that our great Medicine had not overheard their last query, respecting the ''large
green grasshopper''; for, in that case, it might have gone very
hard with them (the Sioux). Our great Medicine was anything but
a large green grasshopper, and *that* they should soon see, to their
cost, if they did not immediately go, the whole of them, about
their business.

Notwithstanding the imminent danger in which we were all
placed, we could scarcely keep our countenances in beholding the
air of profound admiration and astonishment with which the
savages listened to these replies; and I believe that they would
have immediately dispersed, and left us to proceed on our voyage,
had it not been for the unfortunate words in which I informed
them that they were greater rascals than the Ricarees. This was,
apparently, an insult of the last atrocity, and excited them to an

uncontrollable degree of fury. We heard the words "Ricaree! Ricaree!" repeated, every now and then, with the utmost emphasis and excitement; and the whole band, as well as we could judge, seemed to be divided into two factions; the one urging the immense power of the great Medicine, and the other the outrageous insult of being called greater rascals than the Ricarees. While matters stood thus, we retained our position in the middle of the stream, firmly resolved to give the villains a dose of our canistershot, upon the first indignity which should be offered us.

Presently, the interpreter on the grey horse came again into the river, and said that he believed we were no better than we should be; that all the palefaces who had previously gone up the river had been friends of the Sioux, and had made them large presents; that they, the Tetons, were determined not to let us proceed another step unless we came on shore and gave up all our fire-guns and whiskey, with half of our tobacco; that it was plain that we were allies of the Ricarees (who were now at war with the Sioux), and that our design was to carry them supplies, which we should not do; lastly, that they did not think very much of our great Medicine, for he had told us a lie in relation to the designs of the Tetons, and was positively nothing but a great green grasshopper, in spite of all that we thought to the contrary. These latter words, about the great green grasshopper, were taken up by the whole assemblage as the interpreter uttered them, and shouted out at the top of the voice, that the great Medicine himself might be sure to hear the taunt. At the same time, they all broke into wild disorder, galloping their horses furiously in short circles, using contemptuous and indecent gesticulations, brandishing their spears, and drawing their arrows to the head.

I knew that the next thing would be an attack, and so determined to anticipate it at once, before any of our party were wounded by the discharge of their weapons; there was nothing to be gained by delay, and everything by prompt and resolute action. As soon as a good opportunity presented itself, the word was given to fire, and instantly obeyed. The effect of the discharge was very severe, and answered all our purposes to the full. Six of the Indians were killed, and perhaps three times as many badly wounded. The rest were thrown into the greatest terror and confusion and made off into the prairie at full speed, as we drew up our anchors, after reloading the gun, and pulled boldly in for the shore. By the time we had reached it, there was not an unwounded Teton within sight.

I now left John Greely, with three Canadians, in charge of the boats, landed with the rest of the men, and, approaching a savage who was severely but not dangerously wounded, held a conversation with him, by means of Jules. I told him that the whites were well disposed to the Sioux, and to all the Indian nations; that our sole object in visiting his country was to trap beaver, and see the beautiful region which had been given the red men by the Great Spirit; that when we had procured as many furs as we wished, and seen all we came to see, we should return home; that we had heard that the Sioux, and especially the Tetons, were a quarrelsome race, and that therefore we had brought with us our great Medicine for protection; that he was now much exasperated with the Tetons on account of their intolerable insult in calling him a green grasshopper (which he was not); that I had had great difficulty in restraining him from a pursuit of the warriors who had fled, and from sacrificing the wounded who now lay around us; and that I had only succeeded in pacifying him by becoming personally responsible for the future good behaviour of the savages. At this portion of my discourse the poor fellow appeared much relieved, and extended his hand in token of amity. I took it, and assured him and his friends of my protection as long as we were unmolested, following up this promise by a present of twenty carrots of tobacco, some small hardware, beads, and red flannel, for himself and the rest of the wounded.

While all this was going on, we kept a sharp lookout for the fugitive Sioux. As I concluded making the presents, several gangs of these were observable in the distance, and were evidently seen by the disabled savage; but I thought it best to pretend not to perceive them, and shortly afterwards returned to the boats. The whole interruption had detained us full three hours, and it was

after three o'clock when we once more started on our route. We
made extraordinary haste, as I was anxious to get as far as
possible from the scene of action before night. We had a strong
wind at our back, and the current diminished in strength as we
proceeded, owing to the widening of the stream. We therefore
made great way, and by nine o'clock had reached a large and
thickly wooded island, near the northern bank, and close by the
mouth of a creek. Here we resolved to encamp, and had scarcely
set foot on shore, when one of the Greelys shot and secured a fine
buffalo, many of which were upon the place. After posting our
sentries for the night, we had the hump for supper, with as much
whiskey as was good for us. Our exploit of the day was then freely
discussed, and by most of the men was treated as an excellent
joke; but I could by no means enter into any merriment upon
the subject. Human blood had never, before this epoch, been
shed at my hands; and although reason urged that I had taken the
wisest, and what would no doubt prove in the end the most merci-
ful course, still conscience, refusing to hearken even to reason
herself, whispered pertinaciously within my ear: "It is human
blood which thou hast shed." The hours wore away slowly; I
found it impossible to sleep. At length the morning dawned, and
with its fresh dews, its fresher breezes, and smiling flowers, there
came a new courage and a bolder tone of thought, which enabled
me to look more steadily upon what had been done, and to regard
in its only proper point of view the urgent necessity of the deed.

September 7.   Started early and made great way, with a strong
cold wind from the east. Arrived about noon at the upper gorge of
what is called the Great Bend, a place where the river performs a
circuit of full thirty miles, while by land the direct distance is not
more than fifteen hundred yards. Six miles beyond this is a creek
about thirty-five yards wide, coming in from the south. The
country here is of peculiar character; on each side of the river the
shore is strewed thickly with round stones washed from the
bluffs, and presenting a remarkable appearance for miles. The
channel is very shallow, and much interrupted with sand bars.
Cedar is here met with more frequently than any other species of

timber, and the prairies are covered with a stiff kind of prickly pear, over which our men found it no easy matter to walk in their moccasins.

About sunset, in endeavouring to avoid a rapid channel, we had the misfortune to run the larboard side of the large boat on the edge of a sand bar, which so heeled us over that we were very near getting filled with water, in spite of the greatest exertion. As it was, much damage was done to the loose powder, and the Indian goods were all more or less injured. As soon as we found the boat careening, we all jumped into the water, which was here up to our armpits, and by main force held the sinking side up. But we were still in a dilemma, for all our exertions were barely sufficient to keep from capsizing, and we could not spare a man to do anything towards pushing off. We were relieved, very unexpectedly, by the sinking of the whole sand bar from under the boat, just as we were upon the point of despair. The bed of the river in this neighbourhood is much obstructed by these shifting sands, which frequently change situations with great rapidity, and without apparent cause. The material of the bars is a fine hard yellow sand, which, when dry, is of a brilliant glass-like appearance, and almost impalpable.

September 8.   We were still in the heart of the Teton country, and kept a sharp lookout, stopping as seldom as possible, and then only upon the islands, which abounded with game in great variety —buffaloes, elk, deer, goats, black-tailed deer, and antelopes, with plover and brant of many kinds. The goats are uncommonly tame, and have no beard. Fish is not so abundant here as lower down the river. A white wolf was killed by John Greely in a ravine upon one of the smaller islands. Owing to the difficult navigation, and the frequent necessity of employing the tow-line, we did not make great progress this day.

September 9.   Weather growing sensibly colder, which made us all anxious of pushing our way through the Sioux country, as it would be highly dangerous to form our winter encampment in their vicinity. We aroused ourselves to exertion, and proceeded rapidly, the Canadians singing and shouting as we went. Now and then we saw, in the extreme distance, a solitary Teton, but no attempt was made to molest us, and we began to gather courage from this circumstance. Made twenty-eight miles during the day, and encamped at night, in high glee, on a large island well-stocked with game, and thickly covered with cottonwood.

[We omit the adventures of Mr Rodman from this period until the tenth of April. By the last of October, nothing of importance happening in the interval, the party made their way to a small creek which they designated as Otter Creek; and, proceeding up this about a mile to an island well adapted for their purpose, built a log fort and took up their quarters for the winter. The location is just above the old Ricara villages. Several parties of these Indians visited the *voyageurs,* and behaved with perfect friendliness; they had heard of the skirmish with the Tetons, the result of which hugely pleased them. No further trouble was experienced from any of the Sioux. The winter wore away pleasantly, and without accident of note. On the tenth of April the party resumed their voyage.]

IV

April 10, 1792.   The weather was now again most delicious, and revived our spirits exceedingly. The sun began to have power, and the river was quite free of ice, so the Indians assured us, for a hundred miles ahead. We bade adieu to Little Snake [a chief of the Ricarees who had shown the *voyageurs* many evidences of friendship during the winter] and his band, with unfeigned regret, and set out, after breakfast, on our voyage. Perrine (an agent of the Hudson Bay Fur Company on his way to Petite Côte) accompanied us with three Indians for the first ten miles, when he took leave of us and made his way back to the village, where (as we afterwards heard) he met with a violent death from the hands of a squaw, to whom he offered some insult. Upon parting with the agent, we pushed on vigorously up the river, and made great way, notwithstanding a rapid current. In the afternoon, Thornton, who had been complaining for some days past, was taken seriously ill; so much so that I urged the return of the whole party to the hut, there to wait until he should get better; but he resisted this offer so strongly that I was forced to yield. We made him a comfortable bed in the cabin, and paid him every attention; but he had a raging fever, with occasional delirium, and I was much afraid that we should lose him. In the meantime we still pushed ahead with resolution, and by night had made twenty miles, an excellent day's work.

April 11. Still beautiful weather. We started early, and had a good wind, which aided us greatly; so that, but for Thornton's illness, we should all have been in fine spirits. He seemed to grow much worse, and I scarcely knew how to act. Everything was done for his comfort which could be done; Jules, the Canadian, made him some tea, from prairie herbs, which had the effect of inducing perspiration, and allayed the fever very sensibly. We stopped at night on the mainland to the north, and three hunters went out into the prairie by moonlight, returning at one in the morning, without their rifles, and with a fat antelope.

They related that, having proceeded many miles across the country, they reached the banks of a beautiful rivulet, where they were much surprised and alarmed at discovering a large war-party of the Saonie Sioux, who immediately took them prisoners, and carried them a mile on the other side of the stream to a kind of park, or enclosure, walled with mud and sticks, in which was a large herd of antelopes. These animals were still coming into the park, the gates of which were so contrived as to prevent escape. This was an annual practice of the Indians. In the autumn, the antelopes retire for food and shelter from the prairie to the mountainous regions on the south of the river. In the spring they recross it in great numbers, and are then easily taken by being enticed into a strong enclosure as above described.

The hunters (John Greely, the Prophet, and a Canadian) had scarcely any hope of escape from the clutches of the Indians (who numbered as many as fifty), and had well-nigh made up their minds to die. Greely and the Prophet were disarmed and tied hand

and foot; the Canadian, however, was suffered, for some reason not perfectly understood, to remain unbound, and was only deprived of his rifle, the savages leaving him in possession of his hunter's knife (which, possibly, they did not perceive, as it was worn in a sort of sheath in the side of his legging), and treating him otherwise with a marked difference from their demeanour to the others. This circumstance proved the source of the party's deliverance.

It was, perhaps, nine o'clock at night when they were first taken. The moon was bright but, as the air was unusually cool for the season, the savages had kindled two large fires at a sufficient distance from the park not to frighten the antelopes, who were still pouring into it continually. At these fires they were occupied in cooking their game when the hunters so unexpectedly came upon them from round a clump of trees. Greely and the Prophet, after being disarmed and bound with strong thongs of buffalo hide, were thrown down under a tree at some distance from the blaze; while the Canadian was permitted to seat himself, in charge of two savages, by one of the fires, the rest of the Indians forming a circle round the other and larger one. In this arrangement, the time wore away slowly, and the hunters were in momentary expectation of death; the cords of the two who were bound caused them, also, infinite pain, from the tightness with which they were fastened. The Canadian had endeavoured to hold a conversation with his guards, in the hope of bribing them to release him, but could not make himself understood. About midnight, the congregation around the large fire were suddenly disturbed by the dash of several large antelopes in succession through the midst of the blaze. These animals had burst through a portion of the mud wall which confined them, and, mad with rage and affright, had made for the light of the fire, as is the habit of insects at night in like circumstances. It seems, however, that the Saonies had never heard of any similar feat, of these usually timid creatures, for they were in great terror at the unexpected interruption, and their alarm increased to perfect dismay, as the whole captured herd came rushing and bounding upon them, after the lapse of a minute or so from the outbreak of the first few. The hunters described the scene as one of the most singular nature. The beasts were apparently frantic, and the velocity and impetuosity with which they flew, rather than leaped through the flames, and through the midst of the terrified savages, was said by Greely (a man not in the least prone to exaggerate) to have been not only an imposing but even a terrible spectacle. They carried everything before them in their first plunges; but, having cleared the large fire, they immediately dashed at the small one, scattering the brands and blazing wood about; then returned, as if bewildered, to the large one, and so backwards and forwards until the decline of the fires, when, in small parties, they scampered off like lightning to the woods.

Many of the Indians were knocked down in this furious mêlée, and there is no doubt that some of them were seriously, if not mortally, wounded by the sharp hoofs of the agile antelopes. Some threw themselves flat on the ground, and so avoided injury. The Prophet and Greely, not being near the fires, were in no danger. The Canadian was prostrated at the first onset by a kick which rendered him senseless for some minutes. When he came to himself he was nearly in darkness; for the moon had gone behind a heavy thunder-cloud, and the fires were almost out, or only existed in brands scattered hither and thither. He saw no Indians near him, and instantly arousing himself to escape, made, as well as he could, for the tree where his two comrades were lying. Their thongs were soon cut, and the three set off at full speed in the direction of the river, without stopping to think of their rifles, or of anything beyond present security. Having run for some miles, and finding no one in pursuit, they slackened their pace, and made their way to a spring for a draught of water. Here it was they met with the antelope which, as I mentioned before, they brought with them to the boats. The poor creature lay panting, and unable to move, by the border of the spring. One of its legs was broken, and it bore evident traces of fire. It was no doubt one of the herd which had been the means of deliverance. Had there been even a chance of its recovery the hunters would have spared it in token of their gratitude, but it was miserably injured, so they put it at once out of its misery, and brought it home to the boats, where we made an excellent breakfast upon it next morning.

April 12, 13, 14, and 15. During these four days we kept on our course without any adventure of note. The weather was very pleasant during the middle of the day, but the nights and mornings were exceedingly cold, and we had sharp frosts. Game was abundant. Thornton still continued ill, and his sickness perplexed and grieved me beyond measure. I missed his society very much, and now found that he was almost the only member of our party in whom I could strictly confide. By this I merely mean that he was almost the only one to whom I could, or would, freely unburden my heart, with its wild hopes and fantastic wishes—not that any individual among us was unworthy of implicit faith. On the contrary, we were all like brothers, and a dispute, of any importance, never occurred. One interest seemed to bind all; or rather we appeared to be a band of *voyageurs* without interest in view, mere travellers for pleasure. What ideas the Canadians might have held upon this subject I cannot, indeed, exactly say. These fellows talked a great deal, to be sure, about the profits of the enterprise, and especially about their expected share of it; yet I can scarcely think they cared much for these points, for they were the most simple-minded, and certainly the most obliging set of beings upon the face of the earth. As for the rest of the crew, I have no doubt in the world that the pecuniary benefit to be afforded by the expedition was the last thing upon which they speculated. Some singular evidences of the feeling which more or less pervaded us all occurred during the prosecution of the voyage. Interests, which, in the settlements, would have been looked upon as of the highest importance, were here treated as matters unworthy of a serious word, and neglected, or totally discarded upon the most frivolous pretext. Men who had travelled thousands of miles through a howling wilderness, beset by horrible dangers, and enduring the most heartrending privations for the ostensible purpose of collecting peltries, would seldom take the trouble to secure them when obtained, and would leave behind them without a sigh an entire *cache* of fine beaver skins rather than forego the pleasure of pushing up some romantic-looking river, or penetrating into some craggy and dangerous cavern, for minerals whose use they knew nothing about, and which they threw aside as lumber at the first decent opportunity.

In all this my own heart was very much with the rest of the party; and I am free to say that, as we proceeded on our journey, I found myself less and less interested in the main business of the expedition, and more and more willing to turn aside in pursuit of idle amusement, if indeed I am right in calling by so feeble a name as amusement that deep and most intense excitement with which I surveyed the wonders and majestic beauties of the wilderness. No sooner had I examined one region than I was possessed with an irresistible desire to push forward and explore another. As yet, however, I felt as if in too close proximity to the settlements for the full enjoyment of my burning love of nature and of the unknown. I could not help being aware that some civilized footsteps, although few, had preceded me in my journey; that some eyes before my own had been enraptured with the scenes around me. But for this sentiment, ever obtruding itself, I should no doubt have loitered more frequently on the way, turning aside to survey the features of the region bordering upon the river, and perhaps penetrating deeply, at times, into the heart of the country to the north and south of our route. But I was anxious to go on; to get, if possible, beyond the extreme bounds of civilization; to gaze, if I could, upon those gigantic mountains of which the existence had been made known to us only by the vague accounts of the Indians. These ulterior hopes and views I communicated fully to no one of our party save Thornton. He participated in all my most visionary projects, and entered completely into the spirit of the romantic enterprise which pervaded my soul. I therefore felt his illness as a bitter evil. He grew worse daily, while it was out of our power to render him any effectual assistance.

April 16. Today we had a cold rain with a high wind from the north, obliging us to come to anchor until late in the afternoon. At four o'clock p.m. we proceeded, and made five miles by night. Thornton was much worse.

April 17 and 18. During both these days we had a continuance of raw, unpleasant weather, with the same cold wind from the north. We observed many large masses of ice in the river, which was much swollen and very muddy. The time passed unpleasantly, and we made no way. Thornton appeared to be dying, and I now resolved to encamp at the first convenient spot, and remain until his illness should terminate. We accordingly, at noon this day, drew the boats up a large creek coming in from the south and formed an encampment on the mainland.

April 25. We remained at the creek until this morning, when, to the great joy of us all, Thornton was sufficiently recovered to go on. The weather was fine, and we proceeded gaily through a most lovely portion of the country, without encountering a single Indian, or meeting with any adventure out of the usual course until the last of the month, when we reached the country of the Mandans, or rather of the Mandans, the Minnetarees, and the Ahnahaways; for these three tribes all live in the near vicinity of each other, occupying five villages. Not a great many years ago the Mandans were settled in nine villages, about eighty miles below, the ruins of which we passed without knowing what they were—seven on the west and two on the east of the river; but they were thinned off by the smallpox and their old enemies the Sioux, until reduced to a mere handful, when they ascended to their present position. [Mr R. gives here a tolerably full account of the Minnetarees and Ahnahaways or Wassatoons; but we omit it, as differing in no important particular from the ordinary statements respecting these nations.] The Mandans received us with perfect friendliness, and we remained in their neighbourhood three days, during which we overhauled and repaired the piroque, and otherwise refitted. We also obtained a good supply of hard corn, of a mixed colour, which the savages had preserved through the winter in holes near the front of their lodges. While with the Mandans we were visited by a Minnetaree chief, called Wauke-rassah, who behaved with much civility, and was of service to us in many respects. The son of this chief we engaged to accompany us as interpreter as far as the great fork. We made the father several presents, with which he was greatly pleased.* On the first of May we bade adieu to the Mandans, and went on our way.

May 1. The weather was mild, and the surrounding country began to assume a lovely appearance with the opening vegetation, which was now much advanced. The cottonwood leaves were quite as large as a crown, and many flowers were full blown. The low grounds began to spread out here more than usual, and were well supplied with timber. The cottonwood and common willow, as well as red willow, abounded; with rose bushes in great plenty. Beyond the low grounds on the river, the country extended in one immense plain without wood of any kind. The soil was remarkably rich. The game was more abundant than we had ever yet seen it. We kept a hunter ahead of us on each bank, and today they brought in an elk, a goat, five beavers, and a great number of plovers. The beavers were very tame and easily taken. This animal is quite a *bonne bouche* as an article of food; especially the tail, which is of a somewhat glutinous nature, like the fins of the halibut. A beaver tail will suffice for a plentiful dinner for three men. We made twenty miles before night.

May 2. We had a fine wind this morning, and used our sails until noon, when it became rather too much for us, and we stopped for the day. Our hunters went out and shortly returned with an immense elk whom Neptune had pulled down after a long chase, the animal having been only slightly wounded by a buckshot. He measured six feet in height. An antelope was also caught about dusk. As soon as the creature saw our men, it flew off with the greatest velocity, but after a few minutes stopped, and returned on its steps, apparently through curiosity, then bounded away again. This conduct was repeated frequently, each time the game coming nearer and nearer, until at length it ventured within rifle distance, when a shot from the Prophet brought it down. It was lean and with young. These animals, although of incredible swiftness of foot, are still bad swimmers, and thus frequently fall

*The chief Waukerassah is mentioned by Captains Lewis and Clarke, whom he also visited.

a victim to the wolves, in their attempts to cross a stream. Today made twelve miles.

May 3. This morning we made great headway, and by night had accomplished full thirty miles. The game continued to be abundant. Buffaloes, in vast numbers, lay dead along the shore, and we saw many wolves devouring the carcasses. They fled always at our approach. We were much at a loss to account for the death of the buffaloes, but some weeks afterwards the mystery was cleared up. Arriving at a pass of the river where the bluffs were steep and the water deep at their base, we observed a large herd of the huge beasts swimming across, and stopped to watch their motions. They came in a sidelong manner down the current, and had apparently entered the water from a gorge, about half a mile above, where the bank sloped into the stream. Upon reaching the land on the west side of the river they found it impossible to ascend the cliffs, and the water was beyond their depth. After struggling for some time, and endeavouring in vain to set a foothold in the steep and slippery clay, they turned and swam to the eastern shore, where the same kind of inaccessible precipices presented themselves, and where the ineffectual struggle to ascend was repeated. They now turned a second time, a third, a fourth, and a fifth, always making the shore at very nearly the same places. Instead of suffering themselves to go down with the current in search of a more favourable landing (which might have been found a quarter of a mile below), they seemed bent upon maintaining their position, and, for this purpose, swam with their breasts at an acute angle to the stream, and used violent exertions to prevent being borne down. At the fifth time of crossing, the poor beasts were so entirely exhausted that it was evident they could do no more. They now struggled fearfully to scramble up the bank, and one or two of them had nearly succeeded when, to our great distress (for we could not witness their noble efforts without commiseration), the whole mass of loose earth above caved in, and buried several of them in its fall, without leaving the cliff in better condition for ascent. Upon this the rest of the herd commenced a lamentable kind of lowing or moaning, a sound conveying more of a dismal sorrow and despair than anything which it is possible to imagine, I shall never get it out of my head. Some of the beasts made another attempt to swim the river, struggled a few minutes, and sank, the waves above them being dyed with the red blood that gushed from their nostrils in the death agony. But the greater part, after the moaning described, seemed to yield supinely to their fate, rolled over on their backs, and disappeared. The whole herd was drowned; not a buffalo escaped. Their carcasses were thrown up in half an hour afterwards upon the flat grounds a short distance below, where, but for their ignorant obstinacy, they might so easily have landed in safety.

May 4. The weather was delightful, and, with a fair warm wind from the south, we made twenty-five miles before night. Today Thornton was sufficiently recovered to assist in the duties of the boat. In the afternoon he went out with me into the prairie on the west, where we saw a great number of early spring flowers of a kind never seen in the settlements. Many of them were of a rare beauty and delicious perfume. We saw also game in great variety, but shot none, as we were sure the hunters would bring in more than was wanted for use, and I was averse to the wanton destruction of life. On our way home we came upon two Indians of the Assiniboin nation, who accompanied us to the boats. They had evinced nothing like distrust on the way, but, on the contrary, had been frank and bold in demeanour; we were therefore much surprised to see them, upon coming within a stone's throw of the piroque, turn, both of them, suddenly round, and make off into the prairie at full speed. Upon getting a good distance from us, they stopped and, ascended a knoll which commanded a view of the river. Here they lay on their bellies, and, resting their chins on their hands, seemed to regard us with the deepest astonishment. By the aid of a spyglass I could minutely observe their countenances, which bore evidence of both amazement and terror. They continued watching us for a long time. At length, as if struck with a sudden thought, they arose hurriedly and commenced a rapid flight in the direction from which we had seen them issue at first.

May 5.   As we were getting under way very early this morning, a large party of Assiniboins suddenly rushed upon the boats, and succeeded in taking possession of the piroque before we could make any effectual resistance. No one was in it at the time except Jules, who escaped by throwing himself into the river, and swimming to the large boat, which we had pushed out into the stream. These Indians had been brought upon us by the two who had visited us the day before, and the party must have approached us in the most stealthy manner imaginable, as we had our sentries regularly posted, and even Neptune failed to give any token of their vicinity.

We were preparing to fire upon the enemy when Misquash (the new interpreter—son of Waukerassah) gave us to understand that the Assiniboins were friends and were now making signals of amity. Although we could not help thinking that the highway robbery of our boat was but an indifferent way of evincing friendship, still we were willing to see what these people had to say, and desired Misquash to ask them why they had behaved as they did. They replied with many protestations of regard; and we at length found that they really had no intention of molesting us any further than to satisfy an ardent curiosity which consumed them, and which they now entreated us to appease. It appeared that the two Indians of the day before, whose singular conduct had so surprised us, had been struck with sudden amazement at the sooty appearance of our negro, Toby. They had never before seen or heard of a blackamoor, and it must therefore be confessed that their astonishment was not altogether causeless. Toby, moreover, was as ugly an old gentleman as ever spoke, having all the peculiar features of his race—the swollen lips, large white protruding eyes, flat nose, long ears, double head, pot belly and bow legs. Upon relating their adventure to their companions, the two savages could obtain no credit for the wonderful story, and were about losing caste forever, as liars and double-dealers, when they proposed to conduct the whole band to the boats by way of vindicating their veracity. The sudden attack seemed to have been the mere result of impatience on the part of the still incredulous Assiniboins; for they never afterwards evinced the slightest hostility, and yielded up the piroque as soon as we made them understand that we would let them have a good look at old Toby. The latter personage took the matter as a very good joke, and went ashore at once, *in naturalibus,* that the inquisitive savages might observe the whole extent of the question. Their astonishment and satisfaction were profound and complete. At first they doubted the evidence of their own eyes, spitting upon their fingers and rubbing the skin of the negro to be sure that it was not painted. The wool on the head elicited repeated shouts of applause, and the bandy legs were the subject of unqualified admiration. A jig dance on the part of our ugly friend brought matters to a climax. Wonder was now at its height. Approbation could go no further. Had Toby but possessed a single spark of ambition he might then have made his fortune forever by ascending the throne of the Assiniboins, and reigning as King Toby the First.

This incident detained us until late in the day. After interchanging some civilities and presents with the savages, we accepted the aid of six of the band in rowing us about five miles on our route, a very acceptable assistance, and one for which we did not fail to thank Toby. We made, today, only twelve miles, and encamped at night on a beautiful island which we long remembered for the delicious fish and fowl which its vicinity afforded us. We stayed at this pleasant spot two days, during which we feasted and made merry, with very little care for the morrow, and with very little regard to the numerous beaver which disported around us. We might have taken at this island one or two hundred skins without difficulty. As it was, we collected about twenty. The island is at the mouth of a tolerably large river coming in from the south, and at a point where the Missouri strikes off in a due westerly direction. The latitude is about 48 degrees.

May 8.   We proceeded with fair winds and fine weather, and after making twenty or twenty-five miles, reached a large river coming in from the north. Where it debouches, however, it is very narrow, not more than a dozen yards wide, and appears to be quite choked up with mud. Upon ascending it a short distance, a fine bold stream is seen, seventy or eighty yards wide, and very deep, passing through a beautiful valley, abounding in game. Our new guide told us the name of this river, but I have no memorandum of it.* Robert Greely shot here some geese which build their nests upon trees.

May 9. In many places a little distant from the river banks, today, we observed the ground encrusted with a white substance which proved to be a strong salt. We made only fifteen miles, owing to several petty hindrances, and encamped at night on the mainland, among some clumps of cottonwood and rabbit-berry bushes.

May 10. Today the weather was cold, and the wind strong, but fair. We made great headway. The hills in this vicinity are rough and jagged, showing irregular broken masses of rock, some of which tower to a great height, and appear to have been subject to the action of water. We picked up several pieces of petrified wood and bone; and coal was scattered about in every direction. The river gets very crooked.

May 11. Detained the greater part of the day by squalls and rain. Towards evening it cleared up beautifully with a fair wind, of which we took advantage, making ten miles before encamping. Several fat beavers were caught, and a wolf was shot upon the bank. He seemed to have strayed from a large herd which were prowling about us.

May 12. Landed today at noon, after making ten miles, upon a small steep island, for the purpose of overhauling some of our things. As we were about taking our departure, one of the Canadians, who led the van of the party and was several yards in advance, suddenly disappeared from our view with a loud scream. We all ran forward immediately, and laughed heartily upon finding that our man had only tumbled into an empty *cache,* from which we soon extricated him. Had he been alone, however, there is much room for question if he would have got out at all. We

*Probably White-Earth River.

examined the hole carefully, but found nothing in it beyond a few empty bottles; we did not even see anything serving to show whether French, British, or Americans had concealed their goods there; and we felt some curiosity upon this point.

May 13. Arrived at the junction of the Yellowstone with the Missouri, after making twenty-five miles during the day. Misquash here left us, and returned home.

V

THE CHARACTER OF the country through which we had passed for the last two or three days was cheerless in comparison with that to which we had been accustomed. In general it was more level; the timber being more abundant on the skirts of the stream, with little or none at all in the distance. Wherever bluffs appeared upon the margin we descried indications of coal, and we saw one extensive bed of a thick bituminous nature which very much discoloured the water for some hundred yards below it. The current is more gentle than hitherto, the water clearer, and the rocky points and shoals fewer, although such as we had to pass were as difficult as ever. We had rain incessantly, which rendered the banks so slippery that the men who had the towing lines could scarcely walk. The air, too, was disagreeably chilly, and upon ascending some low hills near the river we observed no small quantity of snow lying in the clefts and ridges. In the extreme distance on our right we had perceived several Indian encampments which had the appearance of being temporary, and had been only lately abandoned. This region gives no indication of any permanent settlement, but appears to be a favourite hunting ground with the tribes in the vicinity, a fact rendered evident by the frequent traces of the hunt, which we came across in every direction. The Minnetarees of the Missouri, it is well known, extend their excursions in pursuit of game as high as the great fork, on the south side; while the Assiniboins go up still higher. Misquash informed us that between our present encampment and the Rocky Mountains we should meet with no lodges except those of the Minnetarees that reside on the lower or south side of the Saskatchawine.

The game had been exceedingly abundant, and in great variety: elk, buffalo, big-horn, mule-deer, bears, foxes, beaver, etc., etc., with wild fowl innumerable. Fish was also plentiful. The width of the stream varied considerably from two hundred and fifty yards to passes where the current rushed between bluffs not more than a hundred feet apart. The face of these bluffs generally was composed of a light yellowish freestone intermingled with burnt earth, pumice stone, and mineral salts. At one point the aspect of the country underwent a remarkable change, the hills retiring on both sides to a great distance from the river, which was thickly interspersed with small and beautiful islands, covered with cottonwood. The low grounds appeared to be very fertile; those on the north wide and low, and opening into three extensive valleys. Here seemed to be the extreme northern termination of the range of mountains through which the Missouri had been passing for so long a time, and which are called the Black Hills by the savages. The change from the mountainous region to the level was indicated by the atmosphere, which now became dry and pure; so much so indeed that we perceived its effects upon the seams of our boats, and our few mathematical instruments.

As we made immediate approach to the forks it came on to rain very hard, and the obstructions in the river were harassing in the extreme. The banks in some places were so slippery, and the clay so soft and stiff, that the men were obliged to go barefooted, as they could not keep on their moccasins. The shores also were full of pools of stagnant water, through which we were obliged to wade, sometimes up to our armpits. Then again we had to scramble over enormous shoals of sharp-pointed flints, which appeared to be the wreck of cliffs that had fallen down *en masse*. Occasionally we came to a precipitous gorge or gully, which it would put us to the greatest labour to pass; and in attempting to push by one of these the rope of the large boat (being old and much worn) gave way and permitted her to be swung round by the current upon a ledge of rock in the middle of the stream, where the water was so deep that we could only work in getting her off by the aid of the piroque, and so were a full six hours in effecting it.

At one period we arrived at a high wall of black rock on the south, towering above the ordinary cliffs for about a quarter of a mile along the stream; after which there was an open plain, and about three miles beyond this again, another wall of a light colour, on the same side, fully two hundred feet high; then another plain or valley, and then still another wall of the most singular appearance arises on the north, soaring in height probably two hundred and fifty feet, and being in thickness about twelve feet, with a very regular artificial character. These cliffs present indeed the most extraordinary aspect, rising perpendicularly from the water. The last mentioned are composed of very white soft sandstone, which readily receives the impression of the water. In the upper portion of them appears a sort of frieze or cornice formed by the intervention of several thin horizontal strata of a white freestone, hard, and unaffected by the rains. Above them is a dark rich soil, sloping gradually back from the water to the extent of a mile or thereabouts, when other hills spring up abruptly to the height of full five hundred feet more.

The face of these remarkable cliffs, as might be supposed, is chequered with a variety of lines formed by the trickling of the rains upon the soft material, so that a fertile fancy might easily imagine them to be gigantic monuments reared by human art, and carved over with hieroglyphical devices. Sometimes there are complete niches (like those we see for statues in common temples) formed by the dropping out bodily of large fragments of the sandstone; and there are several points where staircases and long corridors appear, as accidental fractures in the freestone cornice happen to let the rain trickle down uniformly upon the softer material below. We passed these singular bluffs in a bright moonlight, and their effect upon my imagination I shall never forget. They had all the air of enchanted structures (such as I have dreamed of), and the twittering of myriads of martins, which have built their nests in the holes that everywhere perforate the mass, aided this conception not a little. Besides the main walls there are, at intervals, inferior ones, of from twenty to a hundred feet high, and from one to twelve or fifteen feet thick, perfectly regular in shape, and perpendicular. These are formed of a succession of large black-looking stones, apparently made up of loam, sand, and quartz, and absolutely symmetrical in figure, although of various sizes. They are usually square, but sometimes oblong (always parallelipedal), and are lying one above the other as exactly and with as perfect regularity as if placed there by some mortal mason; each upper stone covering and securing the point of junction between two lower ones, just as bricks are laid in a wall. Sometimes these singular erections run in parallel lines, as many as four abreast; sometimes they leave the river and go back until lost amid the hills; sometimes they cross each other at right angles, seeming to enclose large artificial gardens, the vegetation within which is often of a character to preserve the illusion. Where the walls are thinnest, there the bricks are less in size, and the converse. We regarded the scenery presented to our view at this portion of the Missouri as altogether the most surprising, if not the most beautiful, which we had yet seen. It left upon my own mind an impression of novelty, of singularity, which can never be effaced.

Shortly after reaching the fork we came to a pretty large island on the northern side, one mile and a quarter from which is a low ground on the south very thickly covered with fine timber. After this there were several small islands, at each of which we touched for a few minutes as we passed. Then we came to a very black-looking bluff on the north, and then to two other small islands, about which we observed nothing remarkable. Going a few miles farther we reached a tolerably large island situated near the point of a steep promontory, afterwards passing two others, smaller. All these islands are well timbered. It was at night, on the 13th of May, that we were shown by Misquash the mouth of the large river, which in the settlement goes by the name of the Yellow

Stone, but by the Indians is called the Ahmateaza.* We made our camp on the south shore in a beautiful plain covered with cottonwood.

May 14.   This morning we were awake and stirring at an early hour, as the point we had now reached was one of great importance, and it was requisite that, before proceeding any farther, we should make some survey by way of ascertaining which of the two large streams in view would afford us the best passage onward. It seemed to be the general wish of the party to push up one of these rivers as far as practicable, with a view of reaching the Rocky Mountains, when we might perhaps hit upon the head waters of the large stream Aregan, described by all the Indians with whom we had conversed upon the subject, as running into the great Pacific Ocean. I was also anxious to attain this object, which opened to my fancy a world of exciting adventure, but I foresaw many difficulties which we must necessarily encounter if we made the attempt with our present limited information in respect to the region we should have to traverse, and the savages who occupied it; about which latter we only knew indeed that they were generally the most ferocious of the North American Indians. I was afraid, too, that we might get into the wrong stream, and involve ourselves in an endless labyrinth of troubles which would dishearten the men. These thoughts, however, did not give me any long uneasiness, and I set to work at once to explore the neighbourhood; sending some of the party up the banks of each stream to estimate the comparative volume of water in each, while I myself, with Thornton and John Greely, proceeded to ascend the high grounds in the fork, whence an extensive prospect of the surrounding region might be attained. We saw here an immense and magnificent country spreading out on every side into a vast plain, waving with glorious verdure, and alive with countless herds of buffaloes and wolves, intermingled with occasional elk and antelope. To

*There appears to be some discrepancy here which we have not thought it worth while to alter as, after all, Mr Rodman may not be in the wrong. The Amateaza (according to the narrative of Lewis and Clarke) is the name given by the Minnetarees not to the Yellow Stone, but to the Missouri itself.

the south the prospect was interrupted by a range of high, snow-capped mountains, stretching from southeast to northwest, and terminating abruptly. Behind these again was a higher range, extending to the very horizon in the northwest. The two rivers presented the most enchanting appearance as they wound away their long snake-like lengths in the distance, growing thinner and thinner until they looked like mere faint threads of silver as they vanished in the shadowy mists of the sky. We could glean nothing, from their direction so far, as regards their ultimate course, and so descended from our position much at a loss what to do.

The examination of the two currents gave us but little more satisfaction. The north stream was found to be the deeper, but the south was the wider, and the volume of water differed but little. The first had all the colour of the Missouri, but the latter had the peculiar round gravelly bed which distinguishes a river that issues from a mountainous region. We were finally determined by the easier navigation of the north branch to pursue this course, although from the rapidly increasing shallowness we found that in a few days, at farthest, we should have to dispense with the large boat. We spent three days at our encampment, during which we collected a great many fine skins, and deposited them, with our whole stock on hand, in a well-constructed *cache* on a small island in the river a mile below the junction.* We also brought in a great quantity of game, and especially of deer, some haunches of which we pickled or corned for future use. We found great

Caches are holes very frequently dug by the trappers and fur traders, in which to deposit their furs or other goods during a temporary absence. A dry and retired situation is first selected. A circle about two feet in diameter is then described; the sod within this carefully removed and laid by. A hole is now sunk perpendicularly to the depth of a foot, and afterwards gradually widened until the excavation becomes eight or ten feet deep, and six or seven feet wide. As the earth is dug up, it is cautiously placed on a skin, so as to prevent any traces upon the grass, and, when all is completed, is thrown into the nearest river, or otherwise effectually concealed. This *cache* is lined throughout with dried sticks and hay, or with skins, and within it almost any species of backwoods property may be safely and soundly kept for years. When the goods are in, and well covered with buffalo hide, earth is thrown upon the whole, and stamped firmly down. Afterwards the sod is replaced, and a private mark made upon the neighbouring trees, or elsewhere, indicating the precise location of the depôt.

abundance of the prickly pear in this vicinity, as well as choke-berries in great plenty upon the low grounds and ravines. There were also many yellow and red currants (not ripe), with goose-berries. Wild roses were just beginning to open their buds in the most wonderful profusion. We left our encampment in fine spirits on the morning of May 18.

May 18. The day was pleasant, and we proceeded merrily, notwithstanding the constant interruptions occasioned by the shoals and jutting points with which the stream abounds. The men, one and all, were enthusiastic in their determination to per-severe, and the Rocky Mountains were the sole theme of conver-sation. In leaving our peltries behind us, we had considerably lightened the boats, and we found much less difficulty in getting them forward through the rapid currents than would otherwise have been the case. The river was crowded with islands, at nearly all of which we touched. At night we reached a deserted Indian encampment, near bluffs of a blackish clay. Rattlesnakes dis-turbed us very much, and before morning we had a heavy rain.

May 19. We had not proceeded far before we found the char-acter of the stream materially altered, and very much obstructed by sand bars, or rather ridges of small stones, so that it was with the greatest difficulty we could force a passage for the larger boat. Sending two men ahead to reconnoitre, they returned with an account of a wider and deeper channel above, and once again we felt encouraged to persevere. We pushed on for ten miles and encamped on a small island for the night. We observed a peculiar mountain in the distance to the south, of a conical form, isolated, and entirely covered with snow.

May 20. We now entered into a better channel, and pursued our course with little interruption for sixteen miles, through a clayey country of peculiar character, and nearly destitute of vege-tation. At night we encamped on a very large island, covered with tall trees, many of which were new to us. We remained at this spot for five days to make some repairs in the piroque.

During our sojourn here an incident of note occurred. The banks of the Missouri in this neighbourhood are precipitous, and formed of a peculiar blue clay, which becomes excessively slippery after rain. The cliffs, from the bed of the stream back to the distance of a hundred yards, or thereabouts, form a succession of steep terraces of this clay, intersected in numerous directions by deep and narrow ravines, so sharply worn by the action of water at some remote period of time as to have the appearance of artificial channels. The mouths of these ravines, where they debouche upon the river, have a very remarkable appearance, and look from the opposite bank, by moonlight, like gigantic columns standing erect upon the shore. To an observer from the uppermost terrace the whole descent towards the stream has an indescribably chaotic and dreary air. No vegetation of any kind is seen.

John Greely, the Prophet, the interpreter Jules, and myself started out after breakfast one morning to ascend to the topmost terrace on the south shore for the purpose of looking around us; in short, to see what could be seen. With great labour, and by using scrupulous caution, we succeeded in reaching the level grounds at the summit opposite our encampment. The prairie here differs from the general character of that kind of land in being thickly overgrown for many miles back with cottonwood, rose bushes, red willow, and broad-leaved willow; the soil being unsteady, and at times swampy, like that of the ordinary low grounds; it consists of a black-looking loam, one third sand, and when a handful of it is thrown into water, it dissolves in the manner of sugar, with strong bubbles. In several spots we observed deep incrustations of common salt, some of which we collected and used.

Upon reaching these level grounds we all sat down to rest, and had scarcely done so when we were alarmed by a loud growl immediately in our rear, proceeding from the thick underwood. We started to our feet at once in great terror, for we had left our rifles at the island, that we might be unencumbered in the scramble up the cliffs, and the only arms we had were pistols and knives. We had scarcely time to say a word to each other before two enormous brown bears (the first we had yet encountered during the voyage) came rushing at us open-mouthed from a clump of rose bushes. These animals are much dreaded by the Indians, and with reason, for they are indeed formidable creatures, possessing prodigious strength, with untameable ferocity, and the most wonderful tenacity of life. There is scarcely any way of killing them by a bullet, unless the shot be through the brains, and these are defended by two large muscles covering the side of the fore-head, as well as by a projection of a thick frontal bone. They have been known to live for days with half a dozen balls through the lungs, and even with very severe injuries in the heart. So far we had never met with a brown bear, although often with its tracks in the mud or sand, and these we had seen nearly a foot in length, exclusive of the claws, and full eight inches in width.

What to do was now the question. To stand and fight, with such weapons as we possessed, was madness; and it was folly to think of escape by flight in the direction of the prairie; for not only were the bears running towards us from that quarter, but, at a very short distance back from the cliffs, the underwood of brier bushes, dwarf willow, etc., was so thick that we could not have made our way through it at all, and if we kept our course along the river between the underwood and the top of the cliff, the animals would catch us in an instant; for as the ground was boggy we could make no progress upon it, while the large flat foot of the bear would enable him to travel with ease. It seemed as if these reflections (which it takes some time to embody in words) flashed all of them through the minds of all of us in an instant; for every man sprang at once to the cliffs, without sufficiently thinking of the hazard that lay there.

The first descent was some thirty or forty feet, and not very precipitous; the clay here also partook in a slight degree of the loam of the upper soil; so that we scrambled down with no great difficulty to the first terrace, the bears plunging after us with headlong fury. Arrived here, we had not a moment for hesitation. There was nothing left for us now but to encounter the enraged beasts upon the narrow platform where we stood, or to go over the second precipice. This was nearly perpendicular, sixty or seventy feet deep, and composed entirely of the blue clay which was now saturated with late rains, and as slippery as glass itself. The Canadian, frightened out of his senses, leaped to the edge at once, slid with the greatest velocity down the cliff, and was hurled over the third descent by the impetus of his course. We then lost sight of him, and of course supposed him killed; for we could have no doubt that his terrific slide would be continued from precipice to precipice until it terminated with a plunge over the last into the river, a fall of more than a hundred and fifty feet.

Had Jules not gone in this way it is more than probable that we should all have decided, in our extremity, upon attempting the descent; but his fate caused us to waver, and in the meantime the monsters were upon us. This was the first time in all my life I had ever been brought to close quarters with a wild animal of any strength or ferocity, and I have no scruple to acknowledge that my nerves were completely unstrung. For some moments I felt as if about to swoon, but a loud scream from Greely, who had been seized by the foremost bear, had the effect of arousing me to exertion, and when once fairly aroused I experienced a kind of wild and savage pleasure from the conflict.

One of the beasts, upon reaching the narrow ledge where we stood, had made an immediate rush at Greely, and had borne him to the earth, where he stood over him, holding him with his huge teeth lodged in the breast of his overcoat, which, by the greatest good fortune, he had worn, the wind being chilly. The other, rolling rather than scrambling down the cliff, was under so much headway when he reached our station that he could not stop himself until the one half of his body hung over the precipice; he staggered in a sidelong manner, and his right legs went over while he held on in an awkward way with his two left. While thus situated he seized Wormley by the heel with his mouth, and for an instant I feared the worst, for in his efforts to free himself from the grasp, the terrified struggler aided the bear to regain his footing. While I stood helpless, as above described, through terror, and watching the event without ability to render the slightest aid, the shoe and moccasin of Wormley were torn off in the grasp of the animal, who now tumbled headlong down to the next terrace, but stopped himself, by means of his huge claws, from sliding farther. It was now that Greely screamed for aid, and the Prophet and myself rushed to his assistance. We both fired our pistols at the bear's head; and my own ball, I am sure, must have gone through some portion of his skull, for I held the weapon close to his ear. He seemed more angry, however, than hurt; the only good effect of the discharge was in his quitting his hold of Greely (who had sustained no injury) and making at us. We had nothing but our knives to depend upon, and even the refuge of the terrace below was cut off from us by the presence of another bear there. We had our backs to the cliff, and were preparing for a deadly contest, not dreaming of help from Greely (whom we supposed mortally injured) when we heard a shot, and the huge beast fell at our feet, just when we felt his hot and horribly fetid breath in our faces. Our deliverer, who had fought many a bear in his lifetime, had put his pistol deliberately to the eye of the monster, and the contents had entered the brain.

Looking now downwards, we discovered the fallen bruin making ineffectual efforts to scramble up to us, the soft clay yielding to his claws, and he fell repeatedly and heavily. We tried him with several shots, but did no harm, and resolved to leave him where he was for the crows. I do not see how he could ever have made his escape from the spot. We crawled along the ledge on which we stood for nearly half a mile before we found a practicable path to the prairie above us, and did not get into camp until late in the night. Jules was there all alive, but cruelly bruised; so much so, indeed, that he had been unable to give any intelligible account of his accident or of our whereabouts. He had lodged in one of the ravines upon the third terrace, and had made his way down its bed to the river shore.

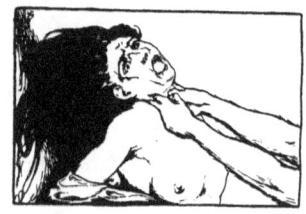

WHO IS THE MURDERER?

Edgar Allan Poe

IN THE SUMMER of the year 1830, there lived at a place called
Eaglescliffe, near Yarm, in the North Riding of Yorkshire, a
man of the name of William Huntley. He was one of the sons of a
respectable farmer who had died about ten years before, leaving
behind him a widow and several children, and considerable property to be divided between them; but his will was so imperfect
and obscure as to have led to a Chancery suit, in order to determine
the true distribution of the property according to his intention—
which was, to leave his widow the interest of a certain sum for her
life, and considerable legacies to each of his children, payable as
they became of age. His son William was, in the year 1830, about
thirty-four years of age, and married, but lived apart from his
wife, with whom he had quarrelled. Owing to his being so long
kept out of his little property, he became a weaver in order to
support himself—and was, in fact, in very humble circumstances.
In point of personal appearance—a matter to which I call your
particular attention—he was of middling stature; he had a broad,
squat face; his head was very large behind; his forehead a retreating one, with rather a deep indentation between the eyebrows;
and he was pitted with the smallpox. But there was one peculiarity
in his face—a very prominent tooth on the left side of the under-
jaw—which caught everyone's eye on first looking at him. It
occasioned him to have a sort of "twist of the mouth"—for
which he had been always known and ridiculed by his companions, even at school.

  The solicitor who had the management of the affairs in Chancery was a Mr Garbutt, residing at Yarm, and still living. He had
occasionally assisted the family, and, amongst them, William
Huntley, by small advances during the time of their being kept out

of their property. At length, on *Thursday, 22nd July 1830*—I also beg your attention to dates—Mr Garbutt was enabled to pay over to him the money due under the will; and on that day gave him a sum of £85.16s.4d.—the balance due after deducting the above-mentioned advances—in seventeen £5 banknotes of the bank of Messrs Backhouse and Company, bankers at Stockton-upon-Tees, and the remainder in silver and copper. He was also entitled to receive other money, which Mr Garbutt had received instructions from him to endeavour to obtain; and I believe that he would have been entitled to a still further sum on his mother's death.

As I have already mentioned, Huntley at this time resided at Eaglescliffe, but was in the constant habit of coming over to a small village at a few miles' distance, called Hutton Rudby, where his mother lived, and also an intimate friend of his, one Robert Goldsborough, whose house, on such occasions, he was in the habit of making his own—always passing the night there. Goldsborough was about Huntley's age; was a widower, with a couple of children, and in very destitute circumstances, having even been in the receipt of parish relief down to within a very few months of the period at which this narrative commences. On the day of Huntley's receiving his money, viz. Thursday, the 22nd July, he went over to Hutton Rudby, and stayed there one or two days, principally in company with his friend Goldsborough. There is some reason to believe that Huntley was desirous of preventing two or three creditors of his from knowing that he had received so considerable a sum of money; and also that he had, about the time in question, intimated to one or two persons a wish to go to America.

He appears to have gone very frequently to and fro, between Hutton Rudby and Eaglescliffe, during the ensuing week. At an early hour, five o'clock, on the morning of *Friday, the 30th July,* he was seen coming to Goldsborough's house; again, about three o'clock in the afternoon of that day, walking on the high road, in company with Goldsborough, and a man named Garbutt; a third time, at eight o'clock in the evening of the same day, sitting in Goldsborough's house; and about ten o'clock that night, he, Goldsborough, and Garbutt, were observed walking together in a cheerful and friendly manner—Goldsborough with a gun in his hand—all apparently bending their steps towards Crathorne Wood, which was close by, on a poaching errand. From that moment to the present, Huntley has never once been seen or heard of.

The circumstance of his disappearance was noticed as soon as six on the ensuing day, Saturday—and his continued absence rapidly increased the suspicion and alarm of the neighbourhood. A quantity of stale-looking blood being seen on the side of the high road, on the ensuing Monday morning, very near the spot where he had been last seen walking with Goldsborough and Garbutt—and also a man's recollecting that, between eleven and twelve o'clock on Friday night, he had heard the report of a gun in Crathorne Wood, added to the circumstance of Huntley's having been seen so frequently in Goldsborough's company, down even to the moment of his sudden disappearance, naturally pointed suspicion at Goldsborough, and anxious enquiries were at once made of him by many persons, to know what had become of Huntley. To one person, a creditor of Huntley's, Goldsborough said, with an easy confident air, that he had set Huntley on the road to Whitby, where he was going to take ship for America. To Whitby instantly went several persons in quest of the missing man, but in vain; no such person had been seen or heard of in that direction, nor was there—nor had there been for some time —in that port any vessel bound for America. The disappointed enquirers returned to Goldsborough, to announce the fruitlessness of their search, when he gave another account of Huntley's movements; namely, that he had set Huntley on the way to Liverpool, there to take ship for America; and a short time afterwards, to another class of enquirers, he told an entirely different story, that he had set Huntley on his way to Bidsdale, to see some friends of his residing there.

All this kindled still more vivid suspicion against him. Constables and others searched his house, and found in it a watch, and various articles of clothing, belonging to Huntley, but none of which he made the least attempt to conceal. When asked to account for his possession of them, he gave inconsistent answers. First, he said that Huntley had given them to him; but, on being reminded how improbable it was that a man so covetous as Huntley should have done so, he said that the fact was that he had lent Huntley money, and, on his going off to America, he had left the articles in question as a security for the repayment of what he owed. In short, Goldsborough was universally supposed to have murdered Huntley. On one occasion he said, without any embarrassment of manner, when taunted on the subject, "You'll all see, by and by, whether he's been murdered!" On another occasion, after following to his door a person who had just quitted it, he said to a man standing near, "That gentleman has been here asking after Huntley, but he'll neither find him at my house, nor at Whitby, nor nowhere else." Confident that the missing man had been murdered, the neighbours, and also the constables, searched far and wide after his body. To a party thus engaged, he once went up and said, impatiently, "You fools! it's no use searching there! Only you give up, and I'll bring Huntley to you in a fortnight!" From some cause or other, these efforts were shortly afterwards discontinued.

Some week or ten days after Huntley's disappearance, Goldsborough was observed sitting opposite a very large fire in his house, reading; and a strong smell was perceived as of woollen burning. "Dear me," said a person to him, "you've a large fire for summer time?" He said he could not sleep, so he was sitting up reading. To another person mentioning the smell of woollen burning, he replied that he had been burning only some old things which he had pulled from under the stairs. At times he appeared disconsolate, and agitated, and very reserved. Again, he was found suddenly in possession of a considerable sum of money—in banknotes, gold and silver—which he rather exhibited with some ostentation than concealed, and this as early as within a day or two after Huntley's disappearance: offering to lend to some persons, and making various purchases for himself. He remained at his house till towards the close of the autumn, when, wearied with the perpetual suspicions and ill-feeling exhibited towards him, he removed to the town of Barnsley, about thirty or forty miles off, and hired a loom of a man, at whose house he took up his abode. When asked what his name was, he replied, "Touch me lightly." He brought with him a good stock of clothes—many of them Huntley's—two watches, and plenty of money, with which he was very liberal. He complained of being out of health, and did no work—his chief amusement being the going out to shoot small birds. Some weeks afterwards he went away, and returned in company with a woman, whom he said he had married —and that she had brought him a sum of £80 for her fortune. On being asked whence he had come, he replied, "from Darlington" —and passed under the name of Robert Towers.

This mysterious disappearance of Huntley, connected as it was with the circumstances above related with reference to Golds- borough, gradually ceased to be the subject of gossip and specula- tion. But it may be asked, Why were not the startling facts of the case made the subject of a formal judicial enquiry? Let me ask another question, however, What proof was there that Huntley had been murdered at all, or that he was even dead? Was it impos- sible—or very improbable—that Goldsborough's account of the matter might be a true one, viz. that Huntley had gone to America, and that Goldsborough was purposely giving contradic- tory accounts of Huntley's movements, to enable him to elude discovery? There was, in fact, no *corpus delicti*—the very first step failed. No lawyer, on the above facts only, would feel himself warranted in recommending the prosecution of Goldsborough for murder, with so serious a chance of an acquittal: in which case, he could never have been again tried as the murderer, however conclusive might be evidence subsequently discovered. "However strong and luminous may be the circumstances, the coincidence of which tends to indicate guilt," observes a distin- guished writer on the law of evidence, Mr Starkie, "they avail nothing, unless the *corpus delicti—the fact that the crime has been actually perpetrated*—shall have been first established. So long as the least doubt exists as to *the act*, there can be no certainty as to the criminal agent.''

Thus, then, matters rested for a period of eleven years—that is, till the 21st June 1841—when a number of workmen were employed by a respectable farmer, a Quaker, named Nellist, in making some alteration in the sides of a *stell*, i.e. a brook or rivulet, dividing a place called Stokesley from another called Seymour. While one of the labouring men, named Robinson, was engaged in cutting into one of the sides of the stell, at a spot where there was a curve or bend in the stream, called Stokesley Beck, and which was about five miles distant from the spot where Huntley, Garbutt, and Goldsborough had been last seen walking together, after turning up two cattle bones, he discovered one belonging to a human body —a shin bone; and presently, within a space of about a yard and a quarter, ''the bones of a Christian'', as he expressed it; in fact, a complete skeleton, with the exception of the feet. The head lay at a distance of a yard from the shin bone. Deeming this rather a curious circumstance, he took out the bones very carefully, and laid them out at length on the side of the stell. They had lain at a depth of about three feet from the surface; and had evidently not been deposited there by digging a hole down from the surface, like a grave, but by hollowing out, or digging a hole in the stell-side, and then thrusting in the body, ''back-side first, and doubled up,'' to use the words of the witness. The soil was tough and clayey; and the spot lay at a distance of about a hundred yards from the high road. This stell was, in fact, not an inconsiderable stream, sometimes subject to overflows; and there was a wooden footbridge over it, a good way higher up the stream. The skull was removed from the earth very carefully by hand. It was filled with earth, and the lower back part of it appeared to have been broken off. The bones having been thus carefully laid out, on Robinson's master, Nr Nellist, arriving at the spot in the evening, he saw them with not a little surprise; and on looking at the skull and jaw bone, particularly noticed *a long projecting tooth on the left side of the lower jaw*. With the exception of two or three, all the teeth were in their sockets, and remained in them till the bones, which had been very damp when first discovered, began to dry, when some of the teeth fell out, and, amongst others, the remarkable and all important tooth in question. Before this had occurred, however, Mr Nellist took home with him, on the same evening, the skull and jaw bone, and kept them, together with the loose teeth, in a pail. They were shortly afterwards, but before the prominent tooth in question had dropped out, seen by various persons; several of whom, on noticing the tooth, at once said that the skull was Huntley's, whom they had known. Mr Nellist committed the skull and teeth, a day or two afterwards, to the care of one Gernon, a constable, who put them into a basket; and having heard of the former suspicions against Goldsborough, whom he also ascertained to be then living under another name at Barnsley, set off of his own accord, carrying with him the bones, to take Goldsborough into custody.

On the evening of the 23rd June, he found Goldsborough sitting in his house alone, without his coat, which hung over a chairback. "I have come," said the constable abruptly, "to take you into custody for the murder of William Huntley, eleven years ago"—on which Goldsborough appeared dreadfully agitated. "Look at this," continued the officer, taking out the shattered skull, and showing it to Goldsborough, "and tell me if it isn't the remains of Huntley?" Goldsborough could not look at it, but his eyes wandered round the room; and with increasing trepidation, and bursting into tears, he exclaimed, "I'm innocent! They may swear my life away if they please, but I never had any clothes, or a watch [the constable had asked him if he had not a watch belonging to Huntley], or anything belonging to Huntley! The last time I ever saw him was on Thursday!" The constable then took him into custody, but released him the next morning, considering the evidence against him not sufficient to warrant his detention, especially as he had arrested Goldsborough on his own responsibility only.

The whole matter was soon, however, brought under the notice of the magistrates, and steps were taken at once to obtain any evidence that might throw light on this long-hidden transaction

—a reward of one hundred pounds being offered, in the usual terms, to anyone who should give such evidence as would lead to the discovery and conviction of the murderer of William Huntley. Shortly afterwards a man of the name of Thomas Groundy was heard making such observations as led to his being taken into custody, and on the 10th of August Goldsborough also was again arrested—having continued ever since in the same house in which he had formerly been seized, at Barnsley—on the charge of having murdered William Huntley; Thomas Groundy being charged as an accessory after the fact. The magistrates having heard all the evidence which had been collected, were of opinion that it was expedient for the ends of justice to permit Groundy to turn king's evidence, as it is called—i.e. to be relieved from the charge against himself, in order to give evidence impeaching his fellow-prisoner. That was done; and the following is a verbatim copy of his deposition—every syllable of which is worthy of notice, in consequence of an extraordinary circumstance which occurred shortly after it had been taken:

Thomas Groundy, being charged before us as an accessory after the fact to the murder by Robert Goldsborough of William Huntley, and being, after the hearing of all the evidence on the part of the prosecution, in the exercise of our discretion, admitted by us at this stage of the proceedings to give evidence against the said Robert Goldsborough, on his oath, saith:

On the Wednesday after William Huntley was missing, Robert Goldsborough came to me, and asked me if I would help him with a bag to Stokesley—he was going to America; and I told him I would go, and we went by Neville's hind house, and then we kept no road, and we went down to yon wood beside the stone bridge. He took me to a bag which was laid upon the ground in the wood, and I laid hold of it, and I found like a man's head, and I asked him what it was—and he stopped about five minutes before he spoke, and he then said, "It is a bad job, it is Huntley—as he was walking by me, I shot him." Then I felt frightened, and wanted to go home, and Goldsborough said, "If you mention it, I'll give you as much." And I said I would not mention it, and I wanted to make off, and I made off. That body was in the wood, within two or three hundred yards from the bridge. It is quite a lonely place. It was a rough place in the wood. Goldsborough never said anything more to me about it, and I was frightened, and durst not mention it to him. It was about hay-time. I knew William Huntley. He had a long tooth, and used to twist his mouth.

Sworn, &c., l4th August 1841.

The mark of
THOMAS + GROUNDY.

Two or three hours afterwards, Groundy hanged himself! He had been placed in a room in York Castle, only to await the arrival of his sureties, who were to be bound with him for his appearance to give evidence at the trial, and had not been left above half an hour before he was found suspended by his neckerchief and braces to one of the iron bars of the window, his knees resting on the floor, and quite dead. He had been in good health and spirits, and perfectly sober, up to the last moment of his being seen alive; having observed, in answer to enquiries, that what he had just been swearing to he had mentioned to two or three persons, whom he named, shortly after the facts had happened. An inquest was held on his body, and a verdict returned of *felo de se*. To return, however—Goldsborough, having heard the whole of the evidence thus adduced against him, including, of course, that of Groundy, voluntarily made and signed the following statement, which also I shall present to you *verbatim*:

On Thursday the 22nd July 1830, William Huntley came to my house, and stopped and talked a while, and asked me to take a walk with him. We took a walk down over the bridge, and through Sir William Foulis's plantation. We sat down on the side of the footpath, in the plantation; and he says, "I want you to look at some papers I have;" and so he pulled them out of his inside coat pocket, one a largish paper, which he had got from Mr Garbutt, and he says, "I have been drawing my money," and said he had drawn £85.16s., and he said, "what is the reason of all this money kept back?" I looked at the paper, and told him what the sums were for. He said he did not want it mentioned to every person, for Dalkin, Robert Moon, and some others, who wanted money of him, would be at him. I told him I had nothing to do with it—I should say nothing about it—so we came home together, and he was backwards and forwards out of our house, and other houses in the town, all the day. He laid with me all night, as he generally used to do when he came to the town. He was backwards and forwards all the next day, and he hired a cart and brought a loom down from Robert Moon's, and sold it to George Farnaby that day, and he stopped all night again, and slept with me, and then he came to Stokesley on the Saturday, and tried me several times to go to America with him. I went with him to Stokesley. We were together awhile at Stokesley on that day, and then we parted, and I never saw him any more until the Thursday following, and he came down to me at Farnaby's shop at Hutton, and called of me out, and pushed me sadly to go to America with him, and I told him I had two children, and I should not leave them, as I was both father and mother to them. So he stopped awhile, and he said if I would not go, he could not force me; but if I would go, I should share with him as long as he had a halfpenny. I refused, and he stopped on a while, and we went out, and I set him down a few yards from the door, and left him. We shaked hands and parted; and he said, if Mr Garbutt did not put it out about his money, he would stop a few days longer, if people did not get to know about it. I have no more to say about it. That was the very last time I clapped my eyes upon him. If it was the last words I had to speak, I never was in Crathorne Woods, nor Weary Bank Woods, with Thomas Groundy. You may think it's a lie; but if it were the last words I had to speak, I never was with him.

ROBERT GOLDSBOROUGH.

He was then committed to York Castle, to take his trial at the next spring assizes for Yorkshire—an occasion looked forward to with universal interest by the inhabitants of that great county. Accordingly, at nine o'clock on Wednesday morning, the 9th of March 1842, he made his appearance at the bar of the Crown Court, before Mr Baron Rolfe—than whom a more patient, acute, and clear-headed judge could not have been selected to try such a case—to meet the fearful charge now made against him, of the "wilful murder of William Huntley, by discharging at him a loaded gun, and thereby giving him a mortal wound, of which he instantly died."

"Put up Robert Goldsborough," said the clerk of arraigns to the governor of the castle, as soon as Mr Baron Rolfe had taken his seat; and in a few moments' time a man was led along to the bar of the court, whose appearance instantly excited in me a mixed feeling of pity and suspicion—the latter, however, predominating. He was forty-seven years of age, of average make and height, wearing an old but decent-looking drab greatcoat, a printed cotton neckerchief, clean shirt-collar, and a pair of somewhat tarnished doeskin gloves. His hair and whiskers were of a dull sandy colour; his face rather long and thin; his eyes grey, heavy and slow in their movements, and with a sad expression; his upper lip long and heavy; his mouth compressed, with a certain indication of sullenness and determination. In short, his features were altogether of a rigid cast and a phlegmatic character, wearing an expression of great anxiety and depression. Whatever inward emotion he might be experiencing, he preserved an external composure of manner. On being placed at the bar, he rested his arms on the iron bar, with his hands clasped together—never removing the gloves he wore. This was the attitude which he preserved, with scarce any variation, during the whole of his two days' trial. He pleaded "Not Guilty" with an air of modest firmness and sadness—eyeing each of his jurymen as they were sworn, and also the judge in his imposing ermine robes, and the counsel immediately beneath him, with anxious attention. He appeared to me a man of firm nerves, or rather perhaps of slow feeling, who had made up his mind to the worst. Was he not an object of profound interest? Had he really done the deed which now, after so many years' concealment, was to be dragged into the light of day? Had he shot dead the companion walking beside him in unsuspicious sociality, rifled the bleeding body, and then thrust it, in the dead of the night, into the earth? Or was he standing there as innocent of the crime imputed to him as the judge who was to try him, yet long blighted by unjust suspicion, and now despairing of a fair trial—the miserable victim of blind and cruel prejudice—to be convicted, within a few days hanged, his body buried within the precincts of the prison; and presently afterwards William Huntley to appear again, alive and well!

The counsel for the prosecution opened the case with candour and judgment, giving a very clear account of the facts he expected to be able to establish; and in one of his observations the judge subsequently expressed his anxious concurrence, namely, the necessity there was for the jury to be on their guard against a certain air of romance which seemed shed over the case, and against a secret notion that the guilt of a long-hidden murder was *destined*, by some sort of special providence, to be brought home against the person now charged with it. I shall now proceed to give you a condensed and accurate account of all the *material* facts proved—you keeping your eye, all the while, on any points of coincidence or contradiction that may strike you; and I shall add such observations on the demeanour and character of the witnesses, as may possibly enable you the better to appreciate the value of their evidence. You are already supplied with a key to it, in the brief narrative I have given you in the former part of this article.

At the instance of the prisoner's counsel, all the witnesses were ordered out of court before the counsel opened the case for the prosecution. The following, then, was the evidence adduced to prove, first, that William Huntley *had been* murdered; and secondly, by Robert Goldsborough, the prisoner at the bar.

William Garbutt, a solicitor, proved the facts stated, at the commencement of the narrative, as to the family, the property, the person of William Huntley; particularly the prominent tooth, the payment to him of £85. l6s. 4d. on Thursday the 22nd July 1830. He had examined the skull which had been found, and, from his recollection of the form of Huntley's countenance, believed it to have been his. He had never heard Huntley talk of going to America. A warrant had been issued against Garbutt in 1830, but unsuccessfully, as he had then absconded, and never since been heard of.

George Farnaby had known both Huntley and Goldsborough well. They were very intimate; and the last time he had seen them together was on *Thursday*, 29th July 1830. He saw Goldsborough enter his house (which was in the same yard as the witness's house) about 3 p.m. the next day (*Friday*), with a sort of sack, but could not guess what it contained, nor whether it was light or heavy. On the next evening (*Sunday*), Goldsborough stood at his window, and pressed the witness to accompany him to Yarm fair the next morning, saying, that a man there owed him £5; which sum Goldsborough offered to lend to the witness. Goldsborough went to the fair, and bought a cow there, and put it into a field belonging to witness. A week afterwards I was at Goldsborough's, when Dalkin called to enquire after Huntley. Goldsborough said, Huntley had gone to Whitby to sail for America. The witness had himself heard Huntley speak, at different times, of going to America.

Robert Braithwaite saw Huntley come to Goldsborough's door, knock, and be admitted, about *five o'clock in the morning of Friday, 30th July 1830*. He had a particular tooth in his under jaw, which pushed his lips out. Witness had seen the skull and jaw bone; and the tooth in it corresponded exactly with that of Huntley. Just before his disappearance, witness (a tailor) had made him a dark green coat with yellow roundish buttons, raised in the middle; a yellowish striped waistcoat with yellow buttons; and a pair of patent cord trousers, with a yellow sandy cast, and a broadish rib; and he distinctly observed that Huntley wore those trousers when he called at Goldsborough's, at five o'clock on the Friday morning. Witness had known Goldsborough all his life.

He was always very poor, and unable to pay witness for his clothes without the greatest difficulty.

James Gears was sitting smoking his pipe on the roadside, (where he was engaged breaking stones) at Hutton Rudby, *between three and four o'clock in the afternoon of Friday, 30th July 1830.* Huntley, Goldsborough, and Garbutt came up together, lit their pipes at mine, and then went down the lane, northward, towards Middleton. That was the last time he ever saw Huntley. On *Wednesday, 4th August* 1830, Goldsborough and I were walking together towards some potato fields, and he pulled a quantity of silver out of his left-hand pocket, and four or five £5 banknotes out of his righthand pocket. I knew them by the stamp to be £5 notes. He told me they were Bank of England notes. I said, "Robert, thou's well off—much better than I. I work hard for my family, and yet never have a penny to call my own." He said he had got the money out of the Stockton-on-Tees bank, where he could draw money whenever he wanted it, for he dealt in poultry. He had always till then been very poor; having many times occasion to borrow a little meal and a little flour from the witness. The witness had mentioned the circumstance of the three men lighting their pipes from his, to Bewick the constable, on Monday the 2nd August 1830. [If that were so, he must have then had his suspicions against Goldsborough; and it is rather odd that two days afterwards he should be walking so familiarly with Goldsborough, and should not have challenged him more strictly as to his suddenly acquired wealth. As singular is it that Goldsborough, if guilty, should have so stupidly exhibited it to one who well knew his previous poverty; and that, too, at the very time when everybody was beginning to suspect him as Huntley's murderer.]

James Braithwaite: The last time he ever saw Huntley was about *eight o'clock in the evening of Friday, 30th July 1830*, sitting on a box near the fire-place in Goldsborough's house. His face was full towards witness, who saw him quite plainly. On Monday, 2nd August 1830, was Yarm fair day; and on witness passing along the high road, about nine o'clock in the evening, he observed a pool of blood about fifty yards from the bridge, which is a little below Foxton Bank, on the road from Yarm to Rudby. He mentioned the circumstance the same day to Brigham, the constable. About ten days afterwards, in passing Goldsborough's house about ten o'clock one night, he observed a large fire, and went in, and told Goldsborough that there was a strong smell of woollen burning. He replied that he had been burning some old rags. The witness soon after reminded him that it was bed time, and said, "Aren't you going to bed?" He replied "No; I can't sleep."

James Maw [By far the most important witness in the case. A violent attempt was made to impeach his credit; but in my opinion, and in that of all I conversed with, quite unsuccessfully. He was about forty years old, very calm and collected—with a sort of quaint frankness of manner, and gave his evidence in a fair, straightforward way.]: The last time he had ever seen Huntley was *about nine o'clock on the night of Friday, 30th July 1830*, near the bridle road leading to Crathorne Wood, in company with Goldsborough, who carried a new gun, and Garbutt—all three of whom the witness had long known well. Huntley wore a dark green coat, a yellow neckcloth, (that the witness particularly noticed), and darkish trousers and waistcoat. He spoke to witness, and said, "Where hast thou been, thou caffy dog? [which was a common expression of Huntley's] Wilt go along with us?" "No," replied the witness, "you'll be getting into mischief with your poaching!" "*Do* thou go with us," said Huntley; "we're going to try a new gun, and, if we catch a hare, we'll go to Crathorne, have it stewed, and get some ale." He then pulled out of his pockets some notes, showed them to the witness, and said, "I've plenty of money—I've been to Mr Garbutt's, and drawn part of my fortune." On this, Goldsborough said, "Put up thy money, thou fool; why art exposing it that way?" and then he added (but the witness was not sure whether to Huntley or Garbutt), "We'll have nobody with us." They then went on through the gate on to Crathorne bridle road, and the witness went home, which he reached about ten o'clock. [I shall give the remainder of his evidence in his own words.] "On Saturday, 7th August, Bewick the constable and I

went to the shop of Hall, a butcher at Hutton Rudby, and there
we had some talk about Huntley's being missing; and we and
several others went that night to Goldsborough's house. Bewick
said, 'Goldy, there are strange reports about Huntley; what hast
thou *really* done with him?' Goldsborough was very much
agitated, making no answer for some time; then said he had set
Huntley on the Whitby road as far as Easley Bridge, to take ship
for America. But I said *that* was very unlikely, for there had
been no ship advertised to go to America. Shortly afterwards, he
said he had set Huntley on the Tontine road, to take coach for
Liverpool—which was in the opposite direction to Whitby. I
asked if Huntley had booked at the Tontine? Goldsborough said
no, he had got on the coach beyond the Tontine. On this we all
told him these were two opposite tales. I forget what his answer
was, but he seemed very much agitated—so much so, that he quite
shook, and required to use both his hands to put his hat on.
Bewick and I at another time went to call on him, and found him
walking up and down before some houses near his own. Bewick
said, 'Now, really tell us, what hast thou done with Huntley?' He
answered and said [that was the formal style in which much of the
witness's evidence was given] 'I set him up Carlton Bank, to go
into Bilsdale, to see some friends of his.' We said that was again
another different story; but I forget his answer. The same
evening, I and four other men (some of them constables), who all
died of the cholera when it was here, went to Goldsborough's
house to search it—he not objecting to it. We found a pair of
woollen corded trousers, an old waistcoat, and an old coat. I
could almost have sworn they were all Huntley's. We also found
six new shirts, marked 'W. H. 1', 'W. H. 2', 'W. H. 3',
'W. H. 4', 'W. H. 5', 'W. H. 6', in an old-fashioned piece of
furniture, like a box or press, upstairs; not in the room where one
Hannah Best was engaged washing. The shirts had been made by
one Hannah Butterwick; she was then there, and is now living,
but I know not where. We asked Goldsborough how he explained
all these things; and he said that Huntley had given the things to
him. We said, 'No, no; he's too greedy a man for that,' on which

Goldsborough said he had lent Huntley money, and he had left these things in part payment. There was a watch, seemingly of silver, with 'W. H.' engraved on the back, hanging up over the fireplace. We took it down, and examined it. There were two papers inside, one with the name of 'Mr Needham', the other 'Mr Stephenson, watch and clock-maker, Stokesley'. Goldsborough gave the same account of the watch as he had given of the clothes and shirts. There was a gun up the stairs, like the one I had observed in his hand when I last saw him with Huntley: it was new-looking. His sister-in-law pointed to it, crying and saying, 'Oh, Robert, this is the thing thou'st either killed or hurt Huntley with.' He replied, 'Hold thy tongue, thou fool!' and was much agitated. I afterwards was one of those who went to search for Huntley's body. About fifty yards from that part of the road where the blood was found, near Foxton Bridge, I recollect seeing a place, in a potato ground, where the earth seemed to have been *newly dug*. [It certainly seems most unaccountable that, if this circumstance really had been observed at that time, a spot so challenging suspicion should not have been instantly examined.] After we had been searching some time, we met Goldsborough, who said, 'Where have you been searching to-day?' Several persons replied 'In Foxton Beck, Foxton Woods, and Middleton and Crathorne Woods.' Goldsborough answered, 'He's far more likely to be found in Stokesley Beck.' '' [*The very place where the skeleton was found.*] The witness then described Huntley's face, particularly his projecting tooth; and said he had seen the skull and jaw bone, with the projecting tooth in it, just in the same place as Huntley's was, and projecting in the same way.

John Sanderson lived in a house 200 yards from Crathorne Wood, and well recollected hearing, about eleven or twelve o'clock on the night of Friday, 30th July 1830 (the Friday before Yarm fair), a shot fired in the wood; and a second within about a minute afterwards. It seemed about a quarter of a mile off. He got up and listened; but heard nothing more. There was game in the wood, and there *were* sometimes poachers.

Bartholomew Goldsborough: On going on Monday morning,

2nd August 1830, to Yarm fair, saw a pool of stale-looking blood, about one and a half feet in diameter, lying on the high road (which was not much frequented), a little on the Crathorne side of the road, and in a slanting direction towards the gate leading into Crathorne Wood. He had noticed this blood before he had heard that Huntley was missing. The place where the blood lay was from four to six miles' distance from Stokesley Beck, where the skeleton was found.

Thomas Richardson had sold Goldsborough a single-barrelled gun, on Monday, 26th July 1830, for 8s. It was an old one, but cleaned and polished up so as to look like a new one. He did not pay for it, saying, he would take it on trial. A day or two after Yarm Fair (which was on Monday, 2nd August 1830), the witness called on him for payment. Goldsborough said he would return it—he did not want it, and had not used it. The witness thrust his finger down the muzzle, and when he drew it out it was dirty with the mark of powder. The witness showed him the finger, and told him he *had* used the gun; which the witness then took away. When the witness entered Goldsborough's house, the latter was engaged at a chest, in which were some clothes; he particularly recollected seeing a pair of woollen cord trousers, broad striped, and a yellow cast with them; a yellow waistcoat with a dark stripe, with gilt buttons. There were other clothes of a dark colour. The trousers and waistcoat were Huntley's—for the witness had seen him wear them. He had also seen Huntley wearing a green coat with brass buttons, having a nob on them. [This witness gave his evidence in a satisfactory manner; and admitted, on cross examination, having been once or twice, some time before, imprisoned for poaching, and once for having stolen some goslings; of which, however, he strenuously declared that he had not been guilty. Mr Baron Rolfe, in summing up, seemed to attach no weight to these circumstances as impeaching the value of his evidence.]

Joseph Dalkin: Heard on Sunday, 1st August 1830, of Huntley's disappearance, and went on that day to Goldsborough's, to enquire after him. Goldsborough said he had set Huntley along Stokesley Lane—that he was going to sail for America from

Whitby, at four o'clock on the next morning (Monday.) Witness said he would go and stop him, for he owed witness £4 for a suit of clothes. Goldsborough said, "Huntley and I have had all that matter talked over about his owing thee money; he never intends paying thee—and it's of no use thy going after him." The witness, however, did go immediately to Whitby (a distance of thirty miles) and searched the whole town for Huntley, but in vain: nor was there any vessel going to America. When the witness measured Huntley, he wore a pair of patent cord trousers, with broad rib, and yellowish cast. He had pressed Huntley several times, in vain, to pay his bill.

George Bewick, a linen manufacturer, and also, in 1830, a constable. He had known Huntley, and recollected his disappearance. In consequence of hearing of it, he went soon after to Hall's (the butcher's) shop, where were Goldsborough and several others; but he did not then recollect whether the witness Maw was also there. Huntley's wife also accompanied witness, and he said to Goldsborough, "There's a report that Huntley is missing; and, as I hear you were last with him, I thought you the likeliest person to ask about him." He replied that "Huntley had some relations at Bilsdale, and had gone there to see them." "Why then," asked the witness, "did you tell Joe Dalkin he had gone to Whitby, and thereby give him a sixty miles' journey for nought?" He made some unsatisfactory answer; but what it was the witness did not recollect. He was agitated, and trembled. The witness then said to him, "I understand thou hast Huntley's five shirts: how did'st thou come by them?" He answered that he had bought them of Huntley: to which the witness replied, "I understand you and Huntley bought a web from George Farnaby between you, which made you five shirts each; and it was not likely that either you could buy or he would sell you his five shirts; and here's his wife says he was badly off for shirts—having only a bad one on, and a worse one off!" His answer to this the witness had forgotten. He proceeded to give the same description of Huntley's person which had been given by the other witnesses; adding, "Huntley had something more remarkable about his appearance than most men,'' and that he had seen and examined the skull and jaw bone, and believed it to be Huntley's. [This was an important witness; of respectable character and appearance; and corroborating the evidence of Maw in several most material particulars. No attempt even was made to shake him by cross-examination.]

Anthony Wiles, till within the last seven years, had lived next door to his stepsister, who kept a chandler's shop at Hutton Rudby; and where he had often seen Huntley go in to change his money into half-crown pieces, for which he always seemed to have a peculiar fancy. Witness knew Goldsborough well; and recollected the time of Yarm fair, on Monday, 2nd August 1830. On the Saturday before (31st July) recollected seeing Goldsborough, *Thomas Groundy*, and two others, in a public house drinking, in the front kitchen; they came in about twelve o'clock at night, and remained there till four o'clock in the morning. They had at least thirteen pints of ale; and Goldsborough paid for all—giving half-crowns, and getting change for them every second or third pint. The witness was one of those who had searched for Huntley's body on the Friday or Saturday after he was missing. After having been home to get some refreshment, they returned to their task; and while at a hay stack, which was near about two miles from the place where the bones were found, Goldsborough came up, anxious and breathless, and said, ''What are you doing there?—a lot of fools! If you'll only wait, I'll bring him forward in a fortnight!''

Then was adduced the evidence of the discovery of the bones, and the locality where they were found, of which I have already given some account. The "Stell" in question seemed to be a sort of tributary stream to the river Leven, two or three yards deep, though not very broad, and was occasionally subject to floods, when its water would run very rapidly down, past the spot where the bones were found, which was in a sort of small bend or curve of the stream, where the current had in a manner undermined the bank, which it left considerably overhanging. As I understood it, this hollowed part must have been still further excavated, for the purpose of receiving the body, which was supposed to have been thrust in "backside foremost", leaving the skull at one angle, and the feet at the opposite one of the base of the triangle. The soil was, I believe, alluvial. The spot in question was a very secluded one, being the property of a Colonel——, who had once or twice been seen fishing in it. There was a footbridge, but at a very considerable distance, higher up the stream. The whole of a human skeleton was found except the feet, the small bones of which might have been exposed to the action of the current, and from time to time washed away. All the bones, and particularly the skull, were removed most carefully by the hand, so that no injury might be inflicted by spade or pickaxe. When first discovered, it would appear certain that there was a very prominent tooth on the left of the lower jaw, which arrested the attention of all those who saw it; but soon afterwards, owing to the inconceivable carelessness and stupidity of those entrusted with the custody of such all-important articles, and who permitted every idle visitor to have free access to them, the tooth in question—alas!—was lost! I confess I have seldom experienced such a rising of indignation, as when this disgraceful deficiency of evidence was thus accounted for; and had I been the judge, the very least symptom of my displeasure would have been the disallowance of the costs of any witness in whose custody the bones had been placed when the tooth in question was with them. But to return—it was now nearly five o'clock in the afternoon, and as the case for the crown must inevitably close very shortly, it was very properly determined upon to produce the bones during the broad daylight, to enable the jury, judge and witnesses, to see them distinctly. As soon as I heard a whispered suggestion to that effect, I fixed my eyes closely on the prisoner. As soon as he heard the order given to produce the bones, I perceived that he slightly changed colour; and turning his head a little towards the witness box, where he expected them to be produced, he directed quick furtive glances, while a new square deal box was brought forward, and unlocked. To the eye of a close observer, the prisoner's countenance now evidenced the miserable and almost overpowering agitation he was experiencing—and that, withal, he was nerving himself up, so

to speak, to a great effort. I perceived his breast twice or thrice
heave heavily; and, though conscious of being watched closely by
those around him, he could not keep his eyes for more than a
moment away from the box, with whose mysterious contents he
was to be so quickly confronted. At length a dark brown skull, the
hinder part appearing to have been broken off, was lifted out of
the box: the prisoner's under lip drooped a little, and perceptibly
quivered for a moment or two—and after one or two glances at
the skull, he looked in another direction, his eyes—if I know any
thing of human expression—full of suppressed agony and terror.
Yet again—and again—he glanced at the dumb but fearful witness
produced against him; and from a certain tremulous motion of
the ends of his neckerchief, I could perceive that his heart was
beating violently. Still he never moved from the position which he
had occupied since the morning; though I learnt from one of the
turnkeys who stood near him in the dock, that at the period I am
mentioning, and also at several other periods of the day, he
trembled so violently, and his knees seemed so near giving way,
that they almost thought he would have fallen.

In these observations concerning the prisoner's demeanour,
I am happy to find myself corroborated by a learned friend,
himself a very close observer, who was engaged in the case, and
made a point of watching the prisoner closely at the moment
which I also had selected for so doing. He tells me that he had
also observed another little circumstance—that the prisoner
listened with comparative unconcern to those portions of the
evidence relating to the blood found on the road, the sound of
the gun shot heard in the wood, his possession of the clothes of
Huntley, and his conflicting accounts concerning them and the
movements of Huntley; but whenever there was any allusion to
the disposal of the body, the carrying of it, and depositing it at
Stokesley Beck, he became evidently painfully absorbed by what
was said—agitated and apprehensive—always, however, striving
to conceal his emotion.

For what reason I know not, but no other portions of the skeleton were produced in court than the skull, the jaw bone, the teeth,

and a portion of the pelvis. I examined them all very carefully. They were of a dark brown colour, with no appearance of decay —on the contrary, they seemed strong and compact. Most of the teeth were so loose as to fall out of the sockets, unless held in them while the jaw bone and skull were being examined. None of the teeth were decayed, but were just such as might have been expected in a healthy adult, who had at all events never had diseased teeth. I examined very minutely the socket which had contained, when the bones were first discovered, the prominent tooth—the first molar tooth on the left side of the lower jaw—subsequently so strangely lost. There was little *apparent* difference between it and its corresponding socket on the other side of the lower jaw; than which, however, it was a trifle deeper, and the outside edge projected a little, and only a very little, more outwards. But even had they both been precisely similar, I conceive it yet quite possible that the tooth may, in life, have been a larger one than usual above the gum, and inclining a little outwards, so as to cause a perceptible protrusion of the under lip. As far as my own impression goes, I should certainly have felt the greatest difficulty in pronouncing, from the mere appearance of the socket, that the tooth it had contained must have been such a prominent and projecting one, as to give the living individual a remarkable peculiarity of countenance. But it must be borne in mind that a very striking prominent tooth that socket actually did contain when first removed from the earth, unless all the witnesses who said they observed it, Mr Strother the surgeon included, are perjured, or labouring under an inconceivable delusion on the subject. The skull was dark, and of compact texture; but the first thing that struck you was, that a great portion of the lower hinder part was wanting, and seemed to have been broken off. It had no appearance of having decayed or mouldered away, but of having been fractured, broken off; but whether before or after death, I cannot venture to offer an opinion. The edge was rough and abrupt—I mean not smooth and uniform, but strong and well defined. In short, the missing part *must* have been broken off. I observed no traces whatever of shot marks in any part of the skull or jaw. About two-thirds of the back part of the skull were missing. If one may be allowed to speculate in such a matter, I should say that, if a loaded gun or pistol had been discharged during lifetime at the person to whom that skull had belonged, say with the muzzle pointed at or near either ear, in a direction parallel, or nearly so, with the other; or if, even, it had been discharged from behind, but in a somewhat upward direction; or if the person had been felled by a heavy blow from behind, and subsequently repeated till death ensued; or if, having been in the first instance shot, the back of the head had been battered in by blows from any heavy instrument, whether before or after death —in any of these cases, I should have expected the skull, after lying ten or twelve years in the ground, without having ever been in any coffin, to present the appearance exhibited by the skull in question, while I was handling and examining it in court. But I could by no means say that such an appearance could not also have been occasioned by any violent injury suffered by the skull five, eight, ten, or twelve years after death. It will be observed that the skull in question was found in a tough clayey soil, near a stream, where it may have lain for twelve years, or more, without probably having ever been touched or disturbed since first deposited there; and, when first discovered, was carefully removed by the hand only of him who first saw it. What inference ·is to be drawn from the fact that the skull was found full of earth, but not the sockets of the eyes, nor the mouth, I know not. As to judging from the mere skull of the general form of the countenance during life, it is obviously a matter of infinite difficulty. Who, for instance, can tell whether the party's face was a fat or a lean one? All I can say is, that having heard the same account given by so many of the witnesses of Huntley's face and head, and without regarding their further statement that the skull, in their opinion, had belonged to him, I thought it very probable that such was the fact. The skull was large, particularly towards the back part; the forehead narrow, and rather retreating; there was some sinking between the eyebrows; and from the bones of the nose, I should think it must have been a flat spreading nose.

The only professional witness called, was a respectable surgeon who lived in the neighbourhood where the bones were found. He swore that when he first saw the jaw bone, a day or two after it had been discovered, it contained the remarkable projecting tooth in question; and from the form of the skull, and of the pelvis, he was confident that they had been those of an adult male. He also said, that from the form of the socket, it must have contained such a tooth as would have given Huntley the appearance described by the witnesses. "It is," said he, holding the skull and jaw bone together in his hand, "the skull of a person who had a short round face, a low forehead sloping back, a broad flat nose, and a depression at the top of it." The bones, he continued, appeared to have been in the ground nine or ten years: they *might* have lain there as long even as twenty years; and though certainly much would depend, with reference to such a point, upon the nature of the soil where they had lain, he had not made any chemical examination of it. From the broken appearance of the skull, he pronounced a confident opinion that the person to whom it had belonged had died a violent death. In answer to a pointed question from the judge, the witness repeated that the tooth in question, when he saw it in the jaw, projected a good deal more than such a tooth generally did. So much for the bones.

There was offered in evidence the deposition of Thomas Groundy, and the prisoner's counsel strongly urged that it was inadmissible. The contrary, however, was clear; and Mr Baron Rolfe so held. Groundy had been admitted by the magistrates to give evidence, having been himself thereby exonerated from the charge against him; that evidence had been given on oath, voluntarily, and in the presence of the prisoner, who might have put to him any questions he might have thought proper; the witness was since dead; and his deposition fell within the ordinary rule—being *admissible* in evidence; but what *credit* was due to it, was, of course, quite another matter. The governor of the castle was then sworn, and he proved the fact of Groundy's having been found dead in the manner already described; and then the deposition was formally read in evidence by the officer of the Court.

Mr Garbutt (the first witness, and who was also the clerk to the magistrates) then proved, that as soon as the above deposition had been made, he, accompanied by a police-officer, went to Crathorne Wood, and they found places in it exactly corresponding with those named in the deposition. At the insistance of the prisoner's counsel, Gernon, the officer to whose care the bones had been first committed, was recalled, and produced a flat button which had been found near the bones, and which was of a different description from the buttons which had been spoken of by the witnesses as worn by Huntley—for the purpose, of course, of weakening the evidence of identity. The prisoner's own statement before, on being committed for trial, was then formally put in and read. This closed the case against the prisoner; and it being nearly seven o'clock in the evening, the Court adjourned—the jury being accommodated during the night in the Castle, so that they might enter into conversation with no persons whatever on any pretence.

When the prisoner was placed again at the bar, at nine o'clock on the ensuing morning, his countenance bore marks of the anxiety and agitation he must have endured in the interval, and looked worn and haggard indeed. His counsel then rose, and addressed the jury for three hours, often with considerable force and ingenuity. He impugned the credibility of almost all the witnesses—especially those who had given the strongest evidence. He denied that there was a tittle of evidence to show that Huntley was not at this moment alive and well—and ridiculed the idea of the skull produced being that of Huntley, commenting with just severity on the absence of the tooth—the great point of the pretended identity. His opinion, he said, was, that the bones had belonged to a female; and his "hypothesis" that some drunken person had fallen from the bridge into the stream, been drowned, and the body carried down by the current, and forced into the bend of the stream, where they had been found. He proceeded to argue, at great length and with much vehemence; that the prisoner's possession of Huntley's clothes and property—which he denied to be the fact, for the witnesses "lied"—was consistent with a scheme between him and Huntley to enable the latter to go to America. He said the evidence was a tissue of exaggerations, misrepresentations, and perjuries—the legitimate produce of the "blood money" which had been had recourse to. If Huntley were murdered, again, might it not have been by Garbutt? or Groundy—who had, immediately after his false evidence, gone and hanged himself, like Judas?

He sat down, urging on the jury that it was infinitely better that ten guilty persons should escape, than that one innocent person should be condemned; and Mr Baron Rolfe immediately proceeded to discharge his very responsible and difficult duty of summing up the whole case to the jury. I took no notes of it; and do not, consequently, feel myself warranted in giving any detailed account of so critical a matter, from mere recollection. None of the newspapers have rendered me, in this dilemma, the slightest assistance: for, after giving at great length the speech of the prisoner's counsel (who, of course, must take only one view of the case), the view taken by the judge—the able, experienced, and *impartial* person, on whose view, in nine cases out of ten, adopted by the jury, the prisoner's fate almost exclusively depends in capital charges—is thus summarily dismissed: "Mr Baron Rolfe then proceeded to sum up, commenting on the evidence as he proceeded, and pointing out such facts as bore for or against the prisoner"—but what those facts were, or how dealt with by the judge, the reader of the paper has not the slightest glimmering notion afforded him. If anything said by me could have the least weight with the gentlemen who perform the honourable and responsible duties of reporting cases of law, especially in great criminal trials in the newspapers, I would recommend them to give the *evidence* fully, and also a careful account of the judge's summing up to the jury.

Mr Baron Rolfe's summing up was decidedly adverse to a conviction. He first read over to the jury the whole of the evidence which had been adduced in the case; and then gave a very lucid statement of the principles by which the law required him to be

governed, in estimating the value of that evidence. He left it fairly
to them to judge whether sufficient had been done to satisfy them,
beyond all *reasonable* doubt, that the bones produced were those
of Huntley; but accompanied by a strong expression of his own
opinion, that the evidence was of a very unsatisfactory nature.
Unless they were satisfied on *that* head, there was an end of the
case, for the very first step failed, viz. proving that Huntley was
dead. If, however, on the whole of the facts, they should feel
satisfied in the affirmative, then came the other great question in
the case—had Huntley been murdered by the prisoner at the bar?
Was the evidence strong enough to bring home the charge to him?
His lordship advised them to place little or no reliance on the
evidence contained in Groundy's deposition; and then proceeded
to analyse the *viva voce* evidence which had been given. Even if
the whole of it were believed by the jury, still it was not *absolutely*
inconsistent with the fact of the prisoner's innocence of having
murdered Huntley, and with the truth of his story that he had
assisted Huntley in going off secretly to America. Without
impugning the general character of the witnesses, his lordship
pointed out how unconsciously liable persons were, in cases like
these, to fit facts to preconceived notions, giving them a complexion and a connection not warrantable by the reality—and all this
without *intending* to state what they believed to be untrue. Many
of the facts spoken to were utterly irreconcilable with the supposition of the prisoner's conscious guilt; while others again were
certainly difficult to be accounted for on the supposition of his
innocence. Some were highly improbable, and others inconsistent; while in one or two instances there were material discrepancies between the witnesses: for instance, Maw spoke positively
to seeing *six* shirts, numbered accordingly, up to "W. H. 6",
whereas Bewick proves that there were only *five*—that Huntley
and the prisoner had bought a web sufficient to make them five
shirts apiece. Again, the time and place where the blood was
found—if found it had been—and the two reports of a gun in the
wood, were, especially when coupled with the great distance
at which the bones were found, circumstances very difficult to

connect with the death of Huntley, in the manner suggested by the prosecution. The case, in fact, was distinguished by many singular circumstances—and the duty which thus devolved on the jury was a serious and difficult one, requiring of them calm and unprejudiced consideration. They were to remember that it was for the prosecutor to satisfy them of the guilt of the prisoner—beyond all *reasonable* doubt. If, however, they did entertain serious doubts, then it was their duty to consider the case as *not proved*, or—to use a phrase of which his lordship did not approve—"to give the prisoner *the benefit* of the doubt." Finally, they had sworn to give their verdict *according to the evidence*, and that only. It was their solemn duty to do so, and entirely to disregard any consequences that might follow in their verdict.

The jury then retired from court, attended, as usual, by a sworn bailiff, and taking with them the bones which had been produced in evidence. The prisoner eyed them as they went with deep anxiety, and was then removed from the bar, to await the agitating moment of their return. While he is sitting alone in this frightful suspense, and the jury are engaged in their solemn deliberation, let us endeavour ourselves to deal with this extraordinary case, by considering the principles which our law brings to bear upon such an enquiry—the various solutions of which the facts are susceptible, and which of those solutions we should ourselves be inclined to adopt.

First, then, said the law in this case, in the autumn of 1830— let me be assured of the fact that a murder has been committed— that the missing person is really dead. Melancholy experience warrants the anxiety of the law on this score, namely, to obtain evidence that the missing person is actually dead. The great Lord Hale would never allow a conviction for murder, unless proof were first given of the death of the party charged to have been murdered, by either direct evidence of the fact, or the actual finding of the body; " and this," says he (2 Hale, 290), " for the sake of two cases—the first, one mentioned by my Lord Coke: 'The niece of a gentleman had been heard to cry out, *Good uncle, do not kill me!* and soon afterwards disappeared. He, being presently suspected of having destroyed her for the sake of her property, was required to produce her before the justices of assize. She, however, had absconded, whereby he was unable to produce her; but, thinking to avert suspicion, procured another girl resembling his niece, and produced her as his niece. The fraud was detected, and, together with other circumstances, appeared so strongly to prove the guilt of the uncle, that he was convicted and executed for the supposed murder of his niece, who, as it afterwards turned out, was still living!' '' ''The second case,'' continues Lord Hale, ''happened within my own remembrance in Staffordshire, where one A was long missing; and, upon strong presumptions, B was supposed to have murdered him, and to have consumed him to ashes in an oven, that he might never be found; and upon this, B was indicted for murder, convicted, and executed. Within one year afterwards, A returned, having been indeed sent beyond seas against his will by B, who had thus been innocent of the offence for which he suffered.'' But by far the most remarkable case of this kind on record is that of Ambrose Gwynne, who, on evidence which really appeared conclusive and irresistible, was condemned for murder, hanged and gibbeted; yet, in consequence of a series of singular circumstances, he survived his supposed execution—escaped to a foreign country, and there actually saw and conversed with the very person for the murder of whom he had been condemned to die! Surely the frightful possibility of the recurrence of such cases as these, warrants the law in requiring full and decisive evidence of the death of the party missing. By this, however, is not meant that actual proof of the finding and identifying of the body is absolutely essential. ''To lay down a strict rule to such an extent,'' justly observes Mr Starkie, ''might be productive of the most horrible consequences.'' Accordingly, in Hindmarch's case (2 Leach, 571), a mariner being indicted for the murder of his captain at sea, and a witness swearing that he saw the prisoner throw the captain overboard, and he was never seen or heard of afterwards, it was left to the jury to say whether the deceased had not been killed by the prisoner before being thrown into the sea. The jury found him guilty—with the subsequent unanimous approbation of the twelve judges to whom the case was referred, and the prisoner was executed. It is indeed easy to imagine cases in which the bodies of murdered persons, especially infants, might be removed at once, and for ever, by the murderers, beyond the reach of discovery.

But, to return to the case before us. Where was, in 1830, the *corpus delicti* proof of the fact that a murder had been actually committed? The grounds of *suspicion* were extraordinarily strong; but our law will not convict upon mere suspicion. Then how far was this essential deficiency supplied in 1841, by the discovery of the skeleton, coupled with the additional evidence which that event enabled those engaged in the investigation to collect? First, was that skeleton the skeleton of Huntley? It was a very singular place for a skeleton to have been found in; the position of the bones was curious, to say the least, strongly favouring the notion of the body to which they had belonged having been hastily doubled up and thrust into the earth in the way suggested; the prominent tooth was a most signal token of identity, and as a *fact*, spoken to by several credible witnesses; the general appearance of the skull certainly suited the descriptions of Huntley's countenance and head given by many witnesses; and its battered, broken appearance behind, was, to say the least, a singular circumstance in the case. But I can add nothing to what I have already presented to the reader on this part of the case—and he must judge for himself.

To come next to the testimony of the witnesses. Let me first advert to the circumstance of the reward of one hundred pounds offered for the production of such evidence as should lead to a conviction. Whether or not such a procedure be a politic one? whether calculated to assist or obstruct the progress of justice?— in the one case, by stimulating persons who would otherwise be indifferent, into ferreting out real facts; in the other case, by tempting to the fabrication of false evidence for the sake of gain—I shall not stay to enquire. It is in my opinion a question of importance and difficulty; but one thing is clear—the practice affords a constant topic, under the name of "blood money", for vituperative declamation on the behalf of the most guilty prisoner, and is calculated too often to turn the scale the wrong way—to incline a candid, but anxious juryman, to a distrust of evidence really of the most satisfactory description. Of course, I can speak for myself only; but I believed that all the witnesses intended to speak the truth. I think Mr Baron Rolfe was also of that opinion, though he seemed to suspect that one or two of the witnesses, by long brooding over the matter, had got to put things together which ought not to have been, and even to suppose one or two matters to have happened, which had not. There were certainly discrepancies—but none of a very material description; and could it be otherwise, when such a large body of witnesses came to speak to so many different circumstances, which had happened so long before? An entire concord, in things great and small, would have been a most palpable badge of fraud and falsehood. The circumstance of Huntley's sudden disappearance only the day but one before a particular day, viz. Monday, 2nd August, on which Yarm fair was held, will account for a tolerably minute recollection of what happened about that period; and above all, the attention of the whole neighbourhood was directed, *at the time,* to the circumstances attending so remarkable a disappearance of one of their neighbours and companions. Several of the principal witnesses, moreover, answered promptly in the affirmative to questions put by the prisoner's counsel, manifestly for his advantage—for instance, as to their having heard Huntley talk of going to America, and the absence of all concealment by the prisoner of the clothes, &c., belonging to Huntley. As to the discrepancy with reference to the six shirts spoken of so distinctly and specifically by Maw, while Bewick, whom he described to have been with him at the time, spoke of their being only *five,* and gave a decisive reason for it, with great deference to the judge, I think it deserving of very little consideration. Bewick *corroborates* Maw up to *five* of the shirts, leaving it plain that Maw is under a *bona fide* mistake—after such a lapse of time—as to there having been a sixth. Thus the important fact of the prisoner's being in possession of *five* new shirts belonging to Huntley, is clearly established.

Let me first direct your attention to the *prisoner's own statement*—a matter which, especially when the statement is made deliberately, is always worthy of attention. "In criminal cases," observes the distinguished writer on the Law of Evidence, from whom I have already quoted, "the statement made by the accused is of essential importance in some points of view. Such is the complexity of human affairs, and so infinite the combinations of circumstances, that the true hypothesis which is capable of explaining and reuniting all the apparently conflicting circumstances of the case, may escape the acutest penetration—but the prisoner, so far as he alone is concerned, can always afford a clue to them; and though he may be unable to support his statement by evidence, his account of the transaction is, for this purpose, always most material and important. The effect may be, on the one hand, to suggest a view which consists with the innocence of the accused, and might otherwise have escaped observation; while, on the other hand, its effect may be to narrow the question to the consideration whether that statement be or be not excluded by the evidence." Now, in the present case, the prisoner's statement corroborates a considerable portion of the evidence. He admits a full knowledge, on Thursday, the 22nd July 1830, of Huntley's possession of £85. 16s. 4d., and that Thursday, 29th July 1830, was "the very last time he clapped eyes on" Huntley. Nevertheless, four witnesses speak decisively to the fact of their having seen him in Huntley's company at four different periods of the ensuing memorable day, Friday—viz. 5 o'clock, a.m.; 3 or 4 o'clock, p.m.; 8 o'clock, p.m.; and 9 or 10 o'clock, p.m. —on the last of which occasions, the prisoner (having a gun in his hand), Huntley, and Garbutt being together, and going towards Crathorne Wood, to which they were then very near. Was this a mere error of recollection, or a wilful falsehood of the prisoner's? Or are all the four witnesses contradicting him—each speaking to a different period of the day, and to a different place—in error, or conspirators and perjurers? If they be speaking the truth, it is next to impossible to believe that Goldsborough could have *forgotten* the circumstance of his having been so much in Huntley's company, up even to within an hour or two of his being so mysteriously missing—knowing that his movements in connection with Huntley had immediately become the subject of keen enquiry, and most vehement suspicion. If, then, he deliberately falsified the fact, what are we at liberty to infer from that circumstance, as to his object and motives? Again, before he made the statement, he had heard all the evidence against him read over—and a very essential part of it was that respecting his having been, so very soon after Huntley's disappearance, in possession of his clothes, and also of a large sum of money. Yet he makes no allusion to these matters—neither denies nor accounts for them in any way whatever: and it must not be forgotten that, when arrested by Gernon in June 1841, he denied having ever had any of Huntley's clothes, or his watch. He makes no attempt to account for his sudden possession of so much money between the period of Huntley's disappearance and the spring of 1831—though he did state, *then*, that he had married a wife with *eighty* pounds! Nor does he offer any explanation of the contradictory accounts he had given as to Huntley's having gone to America, and his—the prisoner's —possession of the clothes, &c.; nor re-affirm any of them. In short, his statement appears as remarkable for what it does *not* contain, as it is important for what it *does*. I also consider it characterized by no little tact and circumspection, on the supposition of his guilt: he frankly admits a great deal which he felt he might be contradicted in, if he were to deny it—viz. his knowledge of Huntley's receipt of the exact sum (within a few pence) on the day of his actually receiving it; suggesting a motive for his absconding to America, and for his so frequently being in the prisoner's company—asserting that he finally parted openly with Huntley at the shop door of Farnaby, in the town of Hutton Rudby; and contenting himself with a brief but solemn denial of the truth of Groundy's statement.

That statement, and its author's suicide immediately after making it, invest the whole facts of the case with an air of extraordinary mystery. It contains on the face of it surely a glaring improbability—namely, that the prisoner should have been so insane as to commit himself gratuitously and irretrievably to one who he knew might immediately have caused his apprehension, and secured incontestable proof of his guilt in the murdered body. Stranger still, perhaps, is it, that if Groundy really had no further part in the business than he represents in that statement, he should not have disclosed the guilt of Goldsborough at once, instead of continuing ever after burdened with such a guilty secret, and for no adequate motive. It is to be observed that one of the witnesses, Anthony Wiles, disclosed *incidentally* (for his evidence was called with another view) a circumstance worthy of attention—viz. that one of the men with whom the prisoner was drinking on the Saturday night after Huntley's disappearance, was *Groundy*: yet the prisoner says, "if it was the last words I had to speak, I never was with him." At all events, a faint ray of light is thrown on the case, by the fact that Groundy was actually acquainted with the prisoner, and in his company about the very time of the transaction deposed to. Again, the truth of his description of the localities, is confirmed by those who went to examine them. The prisoner asks him nothing: *was it because he dared not?*

Let us now follow the course of events. I take it to be proved beyond all reasonable doubt, that, contrary to the deliberate signed statement of the prisoner, he was seen with a gun about ten o'clock at night on Friday, 30th July 1830, in company with Huntley and Garbutt, near a lane or bridle road leading to Crathorne Wood. That gun he had purchased only a few days previously, but after his knowledge of the fact of Huntley's receipt of his money. The report of a gun is heard from the wood within an hour or an hour and a half afterwards; Huntley is never seen or heard of any more; and between twelve and one o'clock that night, the prisoner is observed stealing out of his house, to go and listen at the constable's house, and, after being so occupied for a minute or two, return to his own. The next time that he is seen, is when drinking in company with Groundy late on Saturday night. But, on returning for a moment to the wood—it is certainly an embarrassing fact that the witness spoke to having heard *two* reports within half a minute of each other; whereas the prisoner's was a single-barrelled gun. If the witness's recollections were accurate—which I saw no reason whatever to doubt—how is the fact to be accounted for? If the prisoner's was the only gun, it is next to impossible that he could have so rapidly reloaded and fired again, especially under the horrid circumstances supposed. Was there, then, a second gun, which had been unobserved by them, and in Garbutt's hand?—or concealed, in readiness, in the wood?—or had he or the prisoner a *pistol* also, with which to repair an ineffectual first shot?—or was one of the shots fired by a poacher in another part of the wood? However wide of the mark may be all these speculations, there was one fact in evidence respecting this gun which I do not recollect Mr Baron Rolfe commenting upon to the jury. A day or two after the disappearance of Huntley, Richardson called on the prisoner for payment of this gun, when the prisoner refused, and returned it, saying that he did not want it, *and had not used it*: on which, Richardson put his finger down the muzzle to try it, and drew it back all blackened with discharged powder, and thus convicted him of a falsehood. What inference is to be drawn from this?

Then, as to the blood found on the road, a fact spoken to by two credible witnesses at the trial, one of them having also named it to the constable the same day on which he observed it—was it human blood? If so, it was lying very near the spot where Huntley had last been seen; and, if his blood, it must have been lying there, moreover, two days and two nights—i.e. from Friday midnight, till nine o'clock a.m. on Monday morning. The blood was described as *"stale* looking", and the weather had been fair and dry, but the road was not a much frequented one. It was spoken of by one witness as a "pool"; but if so, it could not have lain there since the Friday night; blood then shed, would have become a dark coagulated mass, possibly covered with dust. Again, on the supposition of its having been Huntley's blood, he must have been murdered on the high road; was that a probable thing, when they were close by the secret shades of Crathorne Wood, to which they were all seen going? May they have gone into the wood? May Huntley have become alarmed at their conduct—made his way out of the wood into the high road, and there received the murderous fire of his assailants? But the spot where the blood lay was, moreover, from four to six miles' distance from Stokesley Beck, where the bones were found. When and by whom was Huntley's body taken to Stokesley Beck? It could not have been taken the same night, at least; it is very highly improbable that such would be the fact, for the prisoner was at his own house between twelve and one o'clock that night; and, according to Groundy's account, the body of Huntley was lying in the wood on Wednesday the 4th August. Where then had it lain between the Friday night and the Wednesday following? In a secret part of the wood, covered up? or had it been buried on the Friday night temporarily, in the potato garth, where Maw said he saw some earth that looked newly dug? I own that I am not satisfied with the last piece of Maw's evidence; for it is hard to believe, that had he really witnessed so suspicious an appearance, at such a spot, after such a supposed tragedy, and when actually in quest of the body, he must have called attention to it, and dug it up. I ought to mention, however, that it did not appear that Maw was then aware of the circumstance of the blood on the road.

Here let me put together two little circumstances in the case, which may suggest a not unimportant inference. It would appear highly probable, assuming the bones to have been Huntley's, that for obvious reasons his body would have been stripped of its clothing, to lessen any subsequent chances of detection. Now, there were no vestiges of clothing found with the bones, and eleven years was not, I should think, a sufficiently long space of time to admit of woollen clothes decaying or mouldering away so entirely, as to leave no trace of them—not even buttons of bone or metal—with the exception of one large flat button, which was found at or near the spot, and not answering to the description of any belonging to Huntley, and possibly there by mere accident. If Huntley had been shot, his clothes must have been stained and steeped in blood, and the safety of the murderers would require

the destruction of such evidences of their guilt. Now, several witnesses speak to the fact of Goldsborough's being seen alone a day
or two after Huntley's disappearance, in his house, late at night,
with a large fire (in the first week of August) burning something
that gave out a strong *"smell of woollen burning"*. May these
have been the bloody clothes of Huntley?

To proceed. The prisoner, seen in Huntley's company up to
within a few hours of his sudden and total disappearance, is seen,
the day but one after, laying out £7 in the purchase of a cow, and
in possession of both banknotes and gold—having been, up to a
very short time before, in the most abject poverty, and even desti-
tution—and, moreover, in possession of a large quantity of
clothes belonging, unquestionably, to the missing man. This of
itself, unexplained, is sufficient to raise a violent presumption of
the prisoner's guilt. But here also great caution is necessary. "If a
horse be stolen from A," says Lord Hale, "and the same day B be
found on him, it is a strong presumption that B stole him. Yet I do
recollect that, before a very learned and wary judge, in such an
instance B was condemned, and executed, at Oxford assizes: and
yet, within two assizes afterwards, C being apprehended for
another robbery, upon his judgment and execution confessed that
he had been the man who stole the horse, and that, being closely
pursued, he desired B, a stranger, to walk his horse for him, while
he turned aside, as he said, for a necessary occasion, and escaped,
and B was apprehended with the horse, and died innocently."

Now, in the present case, here is a man suddenly missing,
known to have been possessed of a considerable sum of money—
the prisoner to have been aware of it—to have been seen in his
company up to almost the last moment before his disappearance
—to become suddenly enriched, having previously been a pauper
—and in possession of very many articles of clothing belonging
to the missing man. All these circumstances point one way; but
then, on the other hand, no attempt is made to conceal his possession of either money or clothes, nor to escape or quit the neighbourhood during the time when suspicion was hottest. Then he
gives certainly contradictory answers concerning the way in which

he became possessed of these matters—but all *may* be reconciled with the story he tells, that the missing man has gone to America, and that he (the prisoner) assisted him, and still seeks to baffle the pursuit of his absent friend. But if the latter story be true, is it probable, is it credible, that Huntley, meditating such an expedition, would first strip himself of all his newly purchased clothes, leave them behind him, and never afterwards come or send to claim them? But all the facts of the case, as fairly and as accurately stated as I know, are now laid before you; and is not this indeed a striking specimen of the importance of, and the difficulties attending, circumstantial evidence?

I shall proceed to propose several hypotheses for your consideration, in order to see whether any of them will reconcile all the circumstances, or which of them will reconcile most of them, and in the most natural manner. "The force of circumstantial evidence, being exclusive in its nature, and the mere coincidence of the hypothesis with the circumstances being, in the abstract, insufficient, unless they exclude every other supposition, it is essential to enquire, with the most scrupulous attention, what other hypotheses there may be agreeing wholly or partially with the facts in evidence. Those which agree even partially with the circumstances are not unworthy of examination, because they lead to a more accurate examination of those facts with which, at first, they might appear to be inconsistent; and it is possible that on a more accurate examination of these facts, their authenticity may be rendered doubtful, or even altogether disproved." The same able writer from whom this passage is quoted, Mr Starkie, has another observation, which also I wish you to take along with you in dealing with the facts of this case.

"To *acquit,* on light, trivial and fanciful suppositions, and remote conjectures, is a virtual violation of the juror's oath; while, on the other hand, he ought not to *condemn*, unless the evidence exclude from his mind all *reasonable* doubt as to the guilt of the accused, and *unless he be so convinced by the evidence, that he would venture to act upon that conviction, in matters of the highest concern and importance to his own interest.*"

First Hypothesis: Huntley really did go off in the way alleged, to America or elsewhere, to avoid his creditors, and also his wife, and be relieved from the burden of supporting her. He may have since died a natural—an accidental—or a violent death, under circumstances depriving him of the opportunity of disposing by will of what he knew was coming to him; and this death may have happened very shortly after his departure. He left the more valuable portions of his clothes and property, and a great portion of his money, in Goldsborough's hands, to be forwarded to him; and Goldsborough acted dishonestly by him, in disposing of the clothes and spending the money. Huntley may be now alive, and meditating a return home.

Second Hypothesis: Huntley is dead, and was murdered by Garbutt, in whose company he had been left by Goldsborough. Garbutt being also pursued by the officers of justice for other offences, hastily absconded, and may now be dead, or abroad.

Third Hypothesis: Groundy was the actual murderer, possibly instigated by Goldsborough; or Goldsborough only subsequently informed by Groundy of the murder, and insisting on receiving a great portion of the money, as the price of his silence. He committed suicide from fear lest his guilt should come out in court, at the trial—through his being unable to stand solemn and public questioning upon the subject. He may have been also partly influenced by remorse at having wrongfully sworn away the life of Goldsborough.

Fourth Hypothesis: Groundy, Garbutt, and Goldsborough, or Groundy and Goldsborough, were all concerned as principals in the murder. The second gun was Groundy's, who joined them in the wood.

Lastly: With reference to the prisoner at the bar, let us enquire more fully, whether his guilt or innocence is more consistent with the proved facts of the case.

If *innocent*, he must stand or fall by his story of Huntley's having left him on his way to America, after in vain pressing Goldsborough to accompany him. It certainly does appear that Huntley had contemplated such a step, and there are other circumstances favouring the notion that Goldsborough and Huntley had been busily concerting a scheme for Huntley's going off privately to America. He was, during the whole of the time between the 22nd and 30th July, incessantly coming over to Goldsborough, and remaining in his company. At five o'clock in the morning of the day of his disappearance, he was seen coming to Goldsborough's house, where he was immediately admitted. They may have arranged that Goldsborough should go and fetch Huntley's things, the same day, from Huntley's to Goldsborough's house, to keep for, or send after, Huntley; in pursuance of which Goldsborough went, and returned with the articles in question in a sack, during the afternoon of the same day. It may have been a part of the arrangement, that Huntley should leave a considerable portion of his money in Goldsborough's hands, for safety's sake—to be remitted as Huntley might want it. Or Goldsborough might have promised and intended to follow him shortly afterwards; but fondness for his children may have kept him back—and he may have determined on playing Huntley false, and appropriating the money and property left with him to his own use, relying on Huntley's not venturing to return, lest he should be saddled with the support of his wife; but if he should return, then resolving to impose on him as much difficulty as possible in claiming his own, by converting his money and articles of furniture, and of farming purchases. His contradictory accounts of Huntley's movements are consistent with his wish to baffle the pursuers of Huntley, by putting them on false scents; and this may serve to explain his light jocular tone in speaking of Huntley's absence, "You'll all see, by and by, whether he's murdered or not." In this view of the case, the blood on the road, the gun shot in the wood, and the burning of clothes soon afterwards, if such facts really happened, have no true connection with each other; and the skull and bones produced, were not the skull and bones of Huntley. Let it, moreover, be borne in mind, that Goldsborough did not attempt any concealment of property or money, or escape —neither after nor before suspicion had settled on him—not even when set at liberty after his arrest in the month of July 1841.

But if the prisoner be *guilty*, let us imagine that, from the time of learning that Huntley had become possessed of so considerable a sum of money, the prisoner had conceived the idea of destroying him in order to obtain that money, and in such a manner as to warrant the belief of the neighbourhood that he had only carried into effect his previously expressed intention of going off to America. That in pursuance of such an intention, Huntley had sent his clothes, &c., on the Friday, to the prisoner's house—that, in short, they formed the contents of the bag, or sack, which the prisoner was seen carrying into his house on the Friday after-noon. That, either alone, or in company with Garbutt or Groundy, he allured Huntley into Crathorne Wood, under the pretext of shooting a hare, and enjoying a pleasant supper together; which Huntley—who might have become loquacious through previous drinking with the prisoner, and possibly Garbutt and Groundy, or one of them—mentioned to Maw, in a merry humour, on meet-ing him on the road, as described by Maw. That he may have been shot, either in the wood, or on the high road, where the blood was found; and his body buried for a while, or concealed in the wood till it could be permanently disposed of. That the prisoner then returned to his own house, and having been, possibly, alarmed by some noise into the suspicion that his motions had been watched, slipped out, shortly afterwards, to ascertain whether there were any gounds for his fears. That he then cleansed himself from any marks of the deed in which he had been engaged, and resolved on the course he should pursue—namely, to give out that he had set Huntley on his way to America. That, finding the current of suspicion setting in more strongly against him than he had antici-pated, he resolved, on due deliberation, distrusting the chance of escaping by flight, to stay and brave it out by a bold and consis-tent adherence to the fiction of Huntley's having gone off secretly to America. That if neither Garbutt nor Groundy had been origi-nally parties to the murder, the prisoner may have taken both, or either, subsequently, into his confidence, to secure his or their assistance in successfully disposing of the body; rewarding him or them by a sum of money, which he might have represented as

being the greater portion of what he had found on the person of
Huntley. That the prisoner, either alone, or assisted by one or
both of these men, afterwards disinterred the body, if temporarily
buried, or removed it from any place where it had lain hid, and
carried it to Stokesley Beck, at night-time, and thrust it, naked,
into a hole they dug into the bank of the Beck, as a place distant,
secluded, and to escape suspicion—bringing home the bloody
clothes, and burning them as soon as possible. That, subsequently, he became agitated, silent, and reserved—tormented by
his own reflections, and terrified by the continued strength of
public suspicion, and the search after Huntley's body. That his
object being to divert the searchers, if possible, from proceeding
towards Stokesley Beck, he conceived himself likely to attain that
end by himself suggesting that the body might be found there—a
bold and desperate expedient, founded on the belief that any
suggestion of that sort by *him*, would certainly be disregarded.
That, finding the search at length abandoned, and the vehemence
of public suspicion to be abating, but yet rendering his continuance at Hutton Rudby troublesome and dangerous, he resolved
to transfer his residence, under a forged name, to Barnsley. That
when, so many years afterwards, so abruptly challenged as the
murderer of Huntley, he was thrown off his guard, so as to forget
the notoriety of his having possessed the clothes and property of
Huntley, and denied that fact to the officer who took him into
custody. That he was dismayed by the appearance of Groundy
against him, and dared not ask him any questions, lest he should
thereby reveal more of the transaction; and, consequently, felt
compelled to content himself with a general denial of Groundy's
statements. That he inwardly shrunk from the frightful spectacle
of the shattered skull, knowing it to be that of Huntley—and that
HORROR looked up at him from these eyeless sockets.

But stay! A sudden stir announces the return, after a long
absence, of the jury; and the crowded court is quickly hushed into
agitated silence, as the jury enter—the foreman carrying with him
the skull and bones; and the prisoner is re-placed at the bar to hear
his doom. The judge has in readiness, but concealed, the black

cap, should it become, within a few moments, his dreadful duty to pronounce sentence of death upon the prisoner. The names of the jury are called over one by one, and the prisoner eyes them with unutterable feelings. Then comes the fearful moment.

Clerk of Arraigns: Gentlemen of the Jury, are you agreed upon your verdict? Do you say that Robert Goldsborough, the prisoner at the bar, is guilty of the murder and felony with which he stands charged, or not guilty?

Foreman: NOT GUILTY.

Clerk of Arraigns: Gentlemen of the Jury, you say that the prisoner at the bar, Robert Goldsborough, is not guilty. That is your verdict; and so you say all? (To the Governor of the Castle) Remove the prisoner from the bar.

The verdict did not seem wholly unexpected by the audience; and it was received in blank silence. The prisoner exhibited no symptoms of satisfaction or exultation on hearing the verdict pronounced; but maintained the same phlegmatic *oppressed* air which he had exhibited throughout. As soon, however, as he was removed from the bar, and before he had quitted the dock, he whispered, with tremulous eagerness, in the ear of the officer, "*Can they try me again, lad?*" "No; thou's clear of it now, altogether," was the reply: on which Goldsborough heaved a very deep sigh, and said, "If they'd put me on my trial in 1830, I could have got plenty to come forward and clear me." Within half an hour afterwards, he was seen dressed as he had appeared at the bar of the court, only that he had his hat on, and carried a small bundle of clothes tied up in a blue and white cotton handkerchief under his arm, walking quietly out of the frowning gates of York Castle, once more a free man, to go whithersoever he chose. He was quickly joined by two mean-looking men; and spent the next hour or so in walking about the town, and looking in to the various shop windows, occasionally followed by a little crowd of boys and others who had recognised him.

How, now, say you candid and attentive reader? Had you been upon the jury, should you have said—*Guilty* or *Not Guilty*?

THE FIRE-FIEND
A Nightmare

Charles D. Gardette

I

In the deepest dearth of midnight,
    while the sad and solemn swell
Still was floating, faintly echoed
    from the forest chapel bell—
Faintly, falteringly floating o'er the sable
    waves of air
That were thro' the midnight rolling, chafed
    and billowy with the tolling—
In my chamber I lay dreaming, by the fire-
    light's fitful gleaming,
And my dreams were dreams foredoomed to care!

II

As the last, long, lingering echo of the
    midnight's mystic chime,
Lifting through the sable billows of the
    thither shore of Time—
Leaving on the starless silence not a token
    nor a trace—
In a quivering sigh departed; from my
    couch in fear I started—

Started to my feet in terror, for my dream's
    phantasmal error
Painted in the fitful fire a frightful,
    fiendish, flaming face!

III

On the red hearth's reddest centre,
    from a blazing knot of oak,
Seemed to gibe and grin this
    phantom when in terror I awoke;
And my slumberous eyelids straining as I
    staggered to the floor,
Still in that dread vision seeming, turned
    my gaze toward the gleaming
Hearth and there—Oh, God! I saw it; and
    from its flaming jaw it
Spat a ceaseless, seething, hissing,
    bubbling, gurgling stream of gore!

IV

Speechless struck with stony silence,
    frozen to the floor I stood,
Till methought my brain was hissing with
    that hissing, bubbling blood;
Till I felt my life stream oozing, oozing
    from those lambent lips;
Till the demon seemed to name me—then
    a wondrous calm o'ercame me,

And my brow grew cold and dewy, with a
      death damp stiff and gluey,
And I fell back on my pillow, in apparent
      soul eclipse.

V

Then as in death's seeming shadow,
      in the icy fall of fear
I lay stricken, came a hoarse and
      hideous murmur to my ear;
Came a murmur like the murmur of
      assassins in their sleep—
Muttering: "Higher! higher! higher! I
      am demon of the Fire!
I am Arch-Fiend of the Fire! and each
      blazing roof's my pyre,
And my sweetest incense is the blood and
      tears my victims weep!

VI

"How I revel on the prairie! how I roar
      among the pines!
How I laugh when from the village o'er
      the snow the red flame shines,
And I hear the shrieks of terror with a life
      in every breath!
How I scream with lambent laughter, as I
      hurl each crackling rafter

Down the fell abyss of fire—until higher!
    higher! higher!
Leap the high priests of my altar, in their
    merry dance of death!

VII

"I am Monarch of the Fire! I am Vassal
    King of Death!
World enriching, with the shadow
    of its doom upon my breath!
With the symbol of Hereafter flaming from
    my fatal face!
I command the Eternal Fire! Higher!
    higher! higher! higher!
Leap my ministering demons, like the
    phantasmagoric lemans
Hugging Universal Nature in their
    hideous embrace!"

VIII

Then a sombre silence shut me in a
    solemn, shrouded sleep,
And I slumbered like an infant in the
    'Cradle of the Deep';
Till the belfry in the forest quivered with
    the matin stroke,
And the martins from the edges of its
    lichen-lidded ledges,

Skimmered through the russet arches,
    where the light in torn files marches,
Like a routed army struggling through the
    serried ranks of oak.

IX

Thro' my ivy-fretted casements,
    filtered in a tremulous note,
From the tall and stately linden
    where the robin swelled his throat—
Querulous, quaker-breasted robin, calling
    quaintly for his mate!
Then I started up unbidden from my
    slumber, nightmare ridden,
With the memory of that dire demon in my
    central fire,
On my eye's interior mirror like the
    shadow of a fate!

X

Ah! the fiendish fire had smouldered to a
    white and formless heap.
And no knot of oak was flaming as it
    flamed upon my sleep;
But around its very centre, where the
    demon face had shone,
Forked shadows seemed to linger, pointing,
    as with spectral anger,

To a Bible, massive, golden, on a table
    carved and olden;
And I bowed and said, ''All power is of
    God—of God alone!''

THE LIGHTHOUSE

Edgar Allan Poe & Robert Bloch

January 1, 1796. This day—my first on the lighthouse—I make this entry in my Diary, as agreed on with De Grät. As regularly as I *can* keep the journal, I will—but there is no telling what may happen to a man all alone as I am—I may get sick or worse. . .

So far well! The cutter had a narrow escape—but why dwell on that, since I am *here*, all safe? My spirits are beginning to revive already, at the mere thought of being—for once in my life at least—thoroughly *alone*; for of course Neptune, large as he is, is not to be taken into consideration as "society". Would to Heaven I had ever found in "society" one half as much *faith* as in this poor dog; in such case I and "society" might never have parted—even for a year. . .

What most surprises me, is the difficulty De Grät had in getting me the appointment—and I a noble of the realm! It could not be that the Consistory had any doubt of my ability to manage the light. *One* man has attended it before now—and got on quite as well as the three that are usually put in. The duty is a mere nothing; and the printed instructions are as plain as possible. It would never have done to let Orndoff accompany me. I should never have made any way with my book as long as he was within reach of me, with his intolerable gossip—not to mention that everlasting meerschaum. Besides, I wish to be *alone*. . .

It is strange that I never observed, until this moment, how dreary a sound that word has—"alone"! I could half fancy there was some peculiarity in the echo of these cylindrical walls—but oh, no!—that is all nonsense. I do believe I am going to get nervous about my insulation. *That* will never do. I have not forgotten De Grät's prophecy. Now for a scramble to the lantern and a good look around to "see what I can see". . . To see what I can see indeed!—not very much. The swell is subsiding a little, I think—but the cutter will have a rough passage home, nevertheless. She will hardly get within sight of the Norland before noon tomorrow—and yet it can hardly be more than 190 or 200 miles.

January 2. I have passed this day in a species of ecstasy that I find it impossible to describe. My passion for solitude could scarcely have been more thoroughly gratified. I do not say *satisfied*; for I believe I should never be satiated with such delight as I have experienced today. . .

The wind lulled after daybreak, and by the afternoon the sea had gone down materially. . . Nothing to be seen with the telescope even, but ocean and sky, with an occasional gull.

January 3. A dead calm all day. Towards evening, the sea looked very much like glass. A few seaweeds came in sight; but besides them absolutely *nothing* all day—not even the slightest speck of cloud. . . Occupied myself in exploring the lighthouse. . . It is a very lofty one—as I find to my cost when I have to ascend its interminable stairs—not quite 160 feet, I should say, from the low-water mark to the top of the lantern. From the bottom *inside* the shaft, however, the distance to the summit is 180 feet at least: thus the floor is 20 feet below the surface of the sea, even at low tide. . .

It seems to me that the hollow interior at the bottom should have been filled in with solid masonry. Undoubtedly the whole would have been thus rendered more *safe*—but what am I thinking about? A structure such as this is safe enough under any circumstances. I should feel myself secure in it during the fiercest hurricane that ever raged—and yet I have heard seamen say that, occasionally, with a wind at South-West, the sea has been known to run higher here than anywhere, with the single exception of the Western opening of the Straits of Magellan.

No mere sea, though, could accomplish anything with this solid iron-riveted wall—which, at 50 feet from high-water mark, is four feet thick, if one inch. The basis on which the structure rests seems to me to be chalk. . .

January 4.   I am now prepared to resume work on my book, having spent this day in familiarizing myself with a regular routine.

My actual duties will be, I perceive, absurdly simple—the light requires little tending beyond a periodic replenishment of the oil for the six-wick burner. As to my own needs, they are easily satisfied, and the exertion of an occasional trip down the stairs is all I must anticipate.

At the base of the stairs is the entrance room; beneath that is twenty feet of empty shaft. Above the entrance room, at the next turn of the circular iron staircase, is my store room which contains the casks of fresh water and the food supplies, plus linens and other daily needs. Above that—again another spiral of those interminable stairs!—is the oil room, completely filled with the tanks from which I must feed the wicks. Fortunately, I perceive that I can limit my descent to the store room to once a week if I choose, for it is possible for me to carry sufficient provisions in one load to supply both myself and Neptune for such a period. As to the oil supply, I need only to bring up two drums every three days and thus insure a constant illumination. If I choose, I can place a dozen or more spare drums on the platform near the light and thus provide for several weeks to come.

So it is that in my daily existence I can limit my movements to the upper half of the lighthouse; that is to say, the three spirals opening on the topmost three levels. The lowest is my ''living room''—and it is here, of course, that Neptune is confined the greater part of the day; here, too, that I plan to write at a desk near the wall-slit that affords a view of the sea without. The second highest level is my bedroom and kitchen combined. Here the weekly rations of food and water are contained in cupboards for that purpose; here, too, is the ingenious stove fed by the selfsame oil that lights the beacon above. The topmost level is the service room giving access to the light itself and to the platform surrounding it. Since the light is fixed, and its reflectors set, there is no need for me ever to ascend to the platform save when replenishing the oil supply or making a repair or adjustment as per the written instructions—a circumstance which may well never arise during my stay here.

Already I have carried enough oil, water and provender to the upper levels to last me for an entire month—I need stir from my two rooms only to replenish the wicks.

For the rest, I am free! utterly free—my time is my own, and in this lofty realm I rule as King. Although Neptune is my only living subject I can well imagine that I am sovereign o'er all I see—ocean below and stars above. I am master of the sun that rises in rubicund radiance from the sea at dawn, emperor of wind and monarch of the gale, sultan of the waves that sport or roar in roiling torrents about the base of my palace pinnacle. I command the moon in the heavens, and the very ebb and flow of the tide does homage to my reign.

But enough of fancies—De Grät warned me to refrain from morbid or from grandiose speculation—now I shall take up in all earnestness the task that lies before me. Yet this night, as I sit before the window in the starlight, the tides sweeping against these lofty walls can only echo my exultation; I am free—and, at last, alone!

January 11.   A week has passed since my last entry in this diary, and as I read it over, I can scarce comprehend that it was I who penned those words.

Something has happened—the nature of which lies unfathomed. I have worked, eaten, slept, replenished the wicks twice. My outward existence has been placid. I can ascribe the alteration in my feelings to naught but some inner alchemy; enough to say that a disturbing change has taken place.

Alone! I, who breathed the word as if it were some mystic incantation bestowing peace, have come—I realize it now—to loathe the very sound of the syllables. And the ghastliness of meaning I know full well.

It is a dismaying, it is a dreadful thing, to be alone. Truly alone, as I am, with only Neptune to exist beside me and by his breathing presence remind me that I am not the sole inhabitant of a blind and senseless universe. The sun and stars that wheel overhead in their endless cycle seem to rush across the horizon unheeding—and, of late, unheeded, for I cannot fix my mind upon them with normal constancy. The sea that swirls or ripples below me is naught but a purposeless chaos of utter emptiness.

I thought myself to be a man of singular self-sufficiency, beyond the petty needs of a boring and banal society. How wrong I was!—for I find myself longing for the sight of another face, the sound of another voice, the touch of other hands whether they offer caresses or blows. Anything, anything for reassurement that my dreams are indeed false and that I am *not*, actually, alone.

And yet I *am*. I am, and I will be. The world is two hundred miles away; I will not know it again for an entire year. And it in turn—but no more! I cannot put down my thoughts while in the grip of this morbid mood.

January 13.   Two more days—two more centuries!—have passed. Can it be less than two weeks since I was immured in this prison tower? I mount the turret of my dungeon and gaze at the horizon; I am not hemmed in by bars of steel but by columns and pillars and webs of wild and raging water. The sea has changed; grey skies have wrought a wizardry so that I stand surrounded by a tumult that threatens to become a tempest.

I turn away, for I can bear no more, and descend to my room. I seek to write—the book is bravely begun, but of late I can bring myself to do nothing constructive or creative—and in a moment I fling aside my pen and rise to pace. To endlessly pace the narrow, circular confines of my tower of torment.

Wild words, these? And yet I am not alone in my affliction—Neptune, Neptune the loyal, the calm, the placid—feels it too.

Perhaps it is but the approach of the storm that agitates him so—for Nature bears closer kinship with the beast. He stays constantly at my side, whining now, and the muffled roaring of the waves without our prison causes him to tremble. There is a chill in the air that our stove cannot dissipate, but it is not cold that oppresses him. . .

I have just mounted to the platform and gazed out at the spectacle of gathering storm. The waves are fantastically high; they sweep against the lighthouse in titanic tumult. These solid walls of stone shudder rhythmically with each onslaught. The churning sea is grey no longer—the water is black, black as basalt and as heavy. The sky's hue has deepened so that at the moment no horizon is visible. I am surrounded by a billowing blackness thundering against me. . .

Back below now, as lightning flickers. The storm will break soon, and Neptune howls piteously. I stroke his quivering flanks, but the poor animal shrinks away. It seems that he fears even my presence; can it be that my own features betray an equal agitation? I do not know—I only feel that I am helpless, trapped here and awaiting the mercy of the storm. I cannot write much longer.

And yet I will set down a further statement. I must, if only to prove to myself that reason again prevails. In writing of my venture up to the platform—my viewing of the sea and sky—I omitted to mention the meaning of a single moment. There came upon me, as I gazed down at the black and boiling madness of the waters below, a wild and wilful craving to become one with it. But why should I disguise the naked truth?—I felt an insane impulse to hurl myself into the sea!

It has passed now; passed, I pray, forever. I did not yield to this perverse prompting and I am back here in my quarters, writing calmly once again. Yet the fact remains—the hideous urge to destroy myself came suddenly, and with the force of one of those monstrous waves.

And what—I force myself to realize—was the meaning of my demented desire? It was that I sought escape, escape from loneliness. It was as if by mingling with the sea and the storm I would no longer be *alone*.

But I defy the elements. I defy the powers of the earth and of the heavens. Alone I am, alone I *must* be—and come what may,

I shall survive! My laughter rises above all your thunder!

So—ye spirits of the storm—blow, howl, rage, hurl your watery weight against my fortress—I am greater than you in all your powers. But wait! Neptune. . .something has happened to the creature—I must attend him.

January 16.   The storm is abated. I am back at my desk now, alone—truly alone. I have locked poor Neptune in the store-room below; the unfortunate beast seems driven out of his wits by the forces of the storm. When last I wrote he was worked into a frenzy, whining and pawing and wheeling in circles. He was incapable of responding to my commands and I had no choice but to literally drag him down the stairs by the scruff of his neck and incarcerate him in the store-room where he could not come to harm. I own that concern for *my* safety was involved—the possibility of being imprisoned in this lighthouse with a mad dog must be avoided.

His howls, throughout the storm, were pitiable indeed, but now he is silent. When last I ventured to gaze into the room I perceived him sleeping, and I trust that rest and calm will restore him to my full companionship as before.

Companionship!

How shall I describe the horrors of the storm I faced *alone*?

In this diary entry I have prefaced a date—January 16—but that is merely a guess. The storm has swept away all track of Time. Did it last a day, two days, three—as I now surmise—a week, or a century? I do *not* know.

I know only an endless raging of waters that threatened, time and again, to engulf the very pinnacle of the lighthouse. I know only an eternity of ebony, an aeon of billowing black composed of sea and sky commingled. I only know that there were times when my own voice outroared the storm—but how can I convey the cause of *that*? There was a time, perhaps a full day, perhaps much longer, when I could not bear to rise from my couch but lay with my face buried in the pillows, weeping like a child. But mine were not the pure tears of childhood innocence—call them, rather, the tears of Lucifer upon the realization of his eternal fall from grace. It seemed to me that I was truly the victim of an endless damnation; condemned forever to remain a prisoner in a world of thunderous chaos.

There is no need to write of the fancies and fantasies which assailed me through those unhallowed hours. At times I felt that the lighthouse was giving way and that I would be swept into the sea. At times I knew myself to be a victim of a colossal plot—I cursed De Grät for sending me, knowingly, to my doom. At times (and these were the worst moments of all) I felt the full force of loneliness, crashing down upon me in waves higher than those wrought by water.

But all has passed, and the sea—and myself—are calm again. A peculiar calmness, this; as I gaze out upon the water there are certain phenomena I was not aware of until this very moment.

Before setting down my observations, let me reassure myself that I am, indeed, *quite* calm; no trace of my former tremors or agitation yet remains. The transient madness induced by the storm has departed and my brain is free of phantasms—indeed, my perceptive faculties seem to be sharpened to an unusual acuity.

It is almost as though I find myself in possession of an additional sense, an ability to analyze and penetrate beyond former limitations superimposed by Nature.

The water on which I gaze is placid once more. The sky is only lightly leaden in hue. But wait—low on the horizon creeps a sudden flame! It is the sun, the Arctic sun in sullen splendour, emerging momentarily from the pall to incarnadine the ocean. Sun and sky, sea and air about me, turn to blood.

Can it be I who but a moment ago wrote of returned, regained sanity? I, who have just shrieked aloud, "Alone!" —and half-rising from my chair, heard the muffled booming echo reverberate through the lonely lighthouse, its sepulchral accent intoning "*Alone!*" in answer? It may be that I am, despite all resolution, going mad; if so, I pray the end comes soon.

January 18. There will be no end! I have conceived a notion, a theory which my heightened faculties soon will test. I shall embark upon an experiment. . .

January 26. A week has passed here in my solitary prison. Solitary?—perhaps, but not for long. The experiment is proceeding. I must set down what has occurred.

The sound of the echo set me to thinking. One sends out one's voice and it comes back. One sends out one's thoughts and— can it be that there is a response? Sounds, as we know, travels in waves and patterns. The emanations of the brain, perhaps, travel similarly. And they are not confined by physical laws of time, space, or *duration*.

Can one's thoughts produce a reply that *materializes*, just as one's voice produces an echo? An echo is a product of a certain vacuum. A thought. . .

Concentration is the key. I have been concentrating. My supplies are replenished, and Neptune—visited during my venture below—seems rational enough, although he shrinks away when I approach him. I have left him below and spent the past week here. Concentration, I repeat, is the key to my experiment.

Concentration, by its very nature, is a difficult task: I addressed myself to it with no little trepidation. Strive but to remain seated quietly with a mind "empty" of all thought, and one finds in the space of a very few minutes that the errant body is engaged in all manner of distracting movement—foot tapping, finger twisting, facial grimacing.

This I managed to overcome after a matter of many hours—my first three days were virtually exhausted in an effort to rid myself of nervous agitation and assume the inner and outer tranquillity of the Indian fakir. Then came the task of "filling" the empty consciousness—filling it completely with *one* intense and concentrated effort of will.

What echo would I bring forth from nothingness? What companionship would I seek here in my loneliness? What was the sign or symbol I desired? What symbolized to me the whole absent world of life and light?

De Grät would laugh me to scorn if he but knew the concept that I chose. Yet I, the cynical, the jaded, the decadent, searched my soul, plumbed my longing, and found that which I most desired—a simple sign, a token of all the earth removed: a fresh and growing flower, a *rose*!

Yes, a simple rose is what I have sought—a rose, torn from its living stem, perfumed with the sweet incarnation of life itself. Seated here before the window I have dreamed, I have mused, I have then concentrated with every fibre of my being upon a *rose*.

My mind was filled with redness—not the redness of the sun upon the sea, or the redness of blood, but the rich and radiant redness of the rose. My soul was suffused with the scent of a rose: as I brought my faculties to bear exclusively upon the image, these walls fell away, the walls of my very flesh fell away, and I seemed to merge in the texture, the odour, the colour, the actual *essence* of a rose.

Shall I write of this, the seventh day, when seated at the window as the sun emerged from the sea, I felt the commanding of my consciousness? Shall I write of rising, descending the stairs, opening the iron door at the base of the lighthouse and peering out at the billows that swirled at my very feet? Shall I write of stooping, of grasping, of holding?

Shall I write that I have indeed descended those iron stairs and returned here with my wave-borne trophy—*that this very day, from waters two hundred miles distant from any shore, I have reached down and plucked a fresh rose?*

January 28.   It has not withered! I keep it before me constantly in a vase on this table, and it is a priceless ruby plucked from dreams. It is real—as real as the howls of poor Neptune, who senses that something odd is afoot. His frantic barking does not disturb me; nothing disturbs me, for I am master of a power greater than earth or space or time. And I shall use this power, now, to bring me the final boon. Here in my tower I have become quite the philosopher: I have learned my lesson well and realize that I do not desire wealth, or fame, or the trinkets of society. My need is simply this—companionship. And now, with the power that is mine to control, I shall have it!

Soon, quite soon, I shall no longer be alone!

January 30.   The storm has returned, but I pay it no heed; nor do I mark the howlings of Neptune, although the beast is now literally dashing himself against the door of the store room. One might fancy that his efforts are responsible for the shuddering of the very lighthouse itself, but no; it is the fury of the Northern gale. I pay it no heed, as I say, but I fully realize that this storm surpasses in extent and intensity anything I could imagine as witness to its predecessor.

Yet it is unimportant; even though the light above me flickers and threatens to be extinguished by the sheer velocity of wind that seeps through these stout walls; even though the ocean sweeps against the foundations with a force that makes solid stone seem flimsy as straw; even though the sky is a single black roaring mouth that yawns low upon the horizon to engulf me.

These things I sense but dimly, as I address myself to the appointed task. I pause now only for food and a brief respite— and scribble down these words to mark the progress of resolution towards an inevitable goal.

For the past several days I have bent my faculties to my will, concentrating utterly and to the uttermost upon the summoning of a Companion.

This Companion will be—I confess it!—a woman; a woman far surpassing the limitations of common mortality. For she is, and must be fashioned, of dreams and longing, of desire and delight beyond the bounds of flesh.

She is the woman of whom I have always dreamed, the One I have sought in vain through what I once presumed, in my ignorance, was the world of reality. It seems to me now that I have always known her, that my soul has contained her presence forever. I can visualize her perfectly—I know her hair, each strand more precious than a miser's gold; the riches of her ivory and alabaster brow, the perfection of her face and form are etched forever in my consciousness. De Grät would scoff that she is but the figment of a dream—but De Grät did not see the rose.

The rose—I hesitate to speak of it—has gone. It was the rose which I set before me when first I composed myself to this new effort of will. I gazed at it intently until vision faded, senses stilled, and I lost myself in the attempt of conjuring up my vision of a Companion.

Hours later, the sound of rising waters from without aroused me. I gazed about, my eyes sought the reassurance of the rose and rested only upon a *foulness*. Where the rose had risen proudly in its vase, red crest rampant upon a living stem, I now perceived only a noxious, utterly detestable strand of ichorous decay. No rose this, but only seaweed; rotted, noisome and putrescent. I flung it away, but for long moments I could not banish a wild presentiment—was it true that I had deceived myself? Was it a weed, and only a weed I plucked from the ocean's breast? Did the force of my thought momentarily invest it with the attributes of a rose? Would anything I called up from the depths—the depths of sea or the depths of consciousness—be *truly* real?

The blessed image of the Companion came to soothe these fevered speculations, and I knew myself saved. There *was* a rose; perhaps my thought had created it and nourished it—only when my entire concentration turned to other things did it depart, or resume another shape. And with my Companion, there will be no need for focussing my faculties elsewhere. She, and she alone, will be the recipient of everything my mind, my heart, my soul possesses. If will, if sentiment, if love are needed to preserve her, these things she shall have in entirety. So there is nothing to fear. Nothing to fear. . .

Once again now I shall lay my pen aside and return to the great task—the task of "creation", if you will—and I shall not fail. The fear (I admit it!) of loneliness is enough to drive me forward to unimaginable brinks. She, and she alone, can save me, shall save me, *must* save me! I can see her now—the golden glitter of her—and my consciousness calls to her to rise, to appear before me in radiant reality. Somewhere upon these storm-tossed seas she *exists*, I know it—and wherever she may be, my call will come to her and she will respond.

January 31.   The command came at midnight. Roused from the depths of the most profound innermost communion by a thunder-clap, I rose as though in the grip of somnambulistic compulsion and moved down the spiral stairs.

The lantern I bore trembled in my hand; its light wavered in the wind, and the very iron treads beneath my feet shook with the furious force of the storm. The booming of the waves as they struck the lighthouse walls seemed to place me within the centre of a maelstrom of ear-shattering sound, yet over the demoniacal din I could detect the frenzied howls of poor Neptune as I passed the door behind which he was confined. The door shook with the combined force of the wind and of his still desperate efforts to free himself—but I hastened on my way, descending to the iron door at the base of the lighthouse.

To open it required the use of both hands, and I set the lantern down at one side. To open it, moreover, required the summoning of a resolution I scarcely possessed—for beyond that door was the force and fury of the wildest storm that ever shrieked across these seething seas. A sudden wave might dash me from the doorway, or, conversely, enter and inundate the lighthouse itself.

But consciousness prevailed; consciousness drove me forward.

I *knew*, I thrilled to the certainty that *she* was without the iron portal—I unbolted the door with the urgency of one who rushes into the arms of his beloved.

The door swung open—blew open—roared open—and the storm burst upon me; a ravening monster of black-mouthed waves capped with white fangs. The sea and sky surged forward as if to attack, and I stood enveloped in Chaos. A flash of light-ning revealed the immensity of utter Nightmare.

I saw it not, for the same flash illumined the form, the

lineaments of *she* whom I sought.

Lightning and lantern were unneeded—her golden glory out-shone all as she stood there, pale and trembling, a goddess arisen from the depths of the sea!

Hallucination, vision, apparition? My trembling fingers sought, and found, their answer. Her flesh was real—cold as the icy waters from whence she came, but palpable and permanent. I thought of the storm, of doomed ships and drowning men, of a girl cast upon the waters and struggling towards the succour of the lighthouse beacon. I thought of a thousand explanations, a thousand miracles, a thousand riddles or reasons beyond ration-ality. Yet only one thing mattered—my Companion was here, and I had but to step forward and take her in my arms.

No word was spoken, nor could one be heard in all that Inferno. No word was needed, for she smiled. Pale lips parted as I held out my arms, and she moved closer. Pale lips parted—and I saw the pointed teeth, set in rows like those of a shark. Her eyes, fishlike and staring, swam closer. As I recoiled, her arms came up to cling, and they were cold as the waters beneath, cold as the storm, cold as death.

In one monstrous moment I *knew*, knew with uttermost certainty, that the power of my will had indeed summoned, the call of my consciousness *had* been answered. But the answer came not from the living, for nothing lived in this storm. I had sent my will out over the waters, but the will penetrates all dimensions, and my answer had come from *below* the waters. *She* was from below, where the drowned dead lie dreaming, and I had awakened her with a horrid life. A life that thirsted, and must drink. . .

I think I shrieked, then, but I heard no sound. Certainly, I did not hear the howls from Neptune as the beast, burst from his prison, bounded down the stairs and flung himself upon the creature from the sea.

His furry form bore her back and obscured my vision; in an instant she was falling backwards, away, into the sea that spawned her. Then, and only then, did I catch a glimpse of the final moment of animation in that which my consciousness had summoned. Lightning seared the sight inexorably upon my soul—the sight of the ultimate blasphemy I had created in my pride. The rose had wilted. . .

The rose had wilted and become seaweed. And now, the golden one was gone and in its place was the bloated, swollen obscenity of a thing long-drowned and dead, risen from the slime and to that slime returning.

Only a moment, and then the waves overwhelmed it, bore it back into the blackness. Only a moment, and the door was slammed shut. Only a moment, and I raced up the iron stairs, Neptune yammering at my heels. Only a moment, and I reached the safety of this sanctuary.

Safety? There is no safety in the universe for me, no safety in a consciousness that could create such horror. And there is no safety here—the wrath of the waves increases with every moment, the anger of the sea and its creatures rises to an inevitable crescendo.

Mad or sane, it does not matter, for the end is the same in either case. I know now that the lighthouse will shatter and fall. I am already shattered, and must fall with it.

There is time only to gather these notes, strap them securely in a cylinder and attach it to Neptune's collar. It may be that he can swim, or cling to a fragment of debris. It may be that a ship, passing by this toppling beacon, may stay and search the waters for a sign—and thus find and rescue the gallant beast.

That ship shall not find me. I go with the lighthouse and go willingly, down to the dark depths. Perhaps—is it but perverted poetry?—I shall join my Companion there forever. Perhaps. . .

The lighthouse is trembling. The beacon flickers above my head and I hear the rush of waters in their final onslaught. There is—yes—a wave, bearing down upon me. It is higher than the tower, it blots out the sky itself, everything. . .

Editor's note: Edgar Allan Poe's original manuscript of "The

Lighthouse" *covered four handwritten pages and ended with the notation for January 3. "I took over from there," Robert Bloch says, "and it gave me no end of satisfaction to help give new life to the very last story from the pen of Poe."*

THE MAD TRIST

Robert Haining

Based on an idea by Edgar Allan Poe

I HAD TAKEN up a position some twenty yards away, next to a small yew tree near the edge of the graveyard. From this vantage point I could observe the service, detached from it and the small group of close relatives whose company I felt unable to share, yet close enough to it to be able to offer my respects to the man with whom I have been so closely involved during his last months. In view of all that he had strived for in life, it seemed a sad tribute that his parting should be marked by such a humble and forlorn gathering. The sense of emptiness pervaded even the words of the priest as his droning voice echoed through the tiny churchyard.

The atmosphere of that solemn occasion absorbed me, and wrapped in my imagined solitude, I began recalling the strange and terrifying events of recent weeks that had brought us both to this dismal place. Yet even as I did so, thinking myself, as I said, to be quite alone, I suddenly realized that someone was standing behind me. I felt a cold breath against my cheek and a gentle nudge as if I had been stalked by a friend who had found amusement in my serious contemplations. I turned quickly.

"Good afternoon," he said solemnly and his eyes, after first focusing on me with some intensity, relaxed and gazed across at the same group of figures that had been holding my attention. "A melancholy hour," he went on, "the moment when all our dreams of immortality are laid to rest."

I smiled at his choice of words. He was a small man, but one of distinguished bearing. I thought that perhaps he too had some connection with the deceased. I turned back to look at the service.

"What brings you to witness this sad event?" It seemed he was not interested in a passing conversation.

"I knew him once," I replied, somewhat irritated by his inquisitiveness.

"But not well enough. Or do you have some reason for being only a distant observer?"

I did not feel inclined to answer his question at that moment, and in any case I did not want to give him any reason to delay his departure, but as I turned to make some appropriate response he whispered,

"Please! I did not wish to interrupt you. It is a moment that will not return. Forgive me."

I thought that as he had now realized the indelicacy of his earlier remarks, he would choose to be on his way. As it was, we stood together in silence, I expecting him to go at any moment, and becoming increasingly irritated by his stubborn refusal to leave me in peace.

Yet the longer the man stayed the more my feelings toward him seemed to mellow. Once again I found myself reflecting on the previous weeks, and on the events that had brought both me and indeed the poor unfortunate, who was the object of this late afternoon ceremony, to this place. The happenings of the last few weeks had weighed heavily upon me before but never more so than now. Was it for that reason I began to think of my companion almost as a Father Confessor? His anonymous, perhaps fleeting presence, offered in some strange way an opportunity for me to unburden my thoughts, to exorcize those spirits that so often plagued me. My solitary life offered few such chances in the normal way. The service was still continuing as I said:

"I suppose in a way I feel partly responsible."

"For the fate of this poor fellow?"

I nodded.

"It was a chance remark, you see. How could I have known that it would have, for him, such dire consequences?"

"Have you met Mr Canning, Roger?"

It was at one of Simon's parties where we first met. I had accepted, after many earlier refusals, an invitation to attend one of Simon Montague's literary parties, which he threw regularly in his large Victorian house near the centre of Bristol. After only half an hour I was feeling ill at ease for I seemed to know nobody, and my conversation, as so often seemed to be the case at such occasions, was proving unable to hold the attention of any of the other guests with whom I had become casually paired.

Sensing my boredom, yet determined not to let me slip quietly away, Simon was trying one last throw.

"William Canning is one of our distinguished local authors on the supernatural. Roger here," he said, presenting my literary credentials to the elderly, distinguished man who was now before me, "is something of an expert on. . .er. . .Edgar Allan Poe, is it, Roger? He's written some articles. You two should have a lot in common."

Simon's voice carried a certain condescension, as if he was barely able to accept that such writing was truly literary. For a moment I almost felt as if the two of us were being isolated from the rest of the gathering and that in due course we might be expected to reveal some aspect of a freakish personality that would explain the source of our curious interests. Such an attitude, if in any sense a true reflection of what Simon was thinking, would however have been quite unworthy of this quiet dignified man, whose white hair and slender build lent an almost aristocratic quality to his appearance.

The introductions made, Simon disappeared and the two of us were suddenly alone, neither quite sure of what to make of the other. As a rule, I had found other writers of the supernatural no more companionable than any other type of author. But I had heard of William Canning and had read one or two of his short stories, stories that had struck me as both intelligent and sensitive, far removed from the normal pattern followed by work of that kind. I knew also that he had not enjoyed great financial success from his writing and that his stylistic appeal was very much restricted to a narrow group of devotees for whom he was something of a cult figure. His mode of life was comfortable if not extravagant; he lived for example in an old house on the outskirts of Bristol near the Clifton Gorge, a house that had remained in the Canning family for many years.

We talked for some time about a new book he was trying to write. Although it was not his first, he was finding the project a difficult one to start, partly he claimed because of its scope and partly because of his age and growing infirmity. It was, in his own words, his "last quest for immortality", a last attempt to attain a goal that, he admitted, had been responsible for first luring him into writing. It seemed a naive confession from a man of his age. As a younger man, I too had dreamed of writing the great novel that would ensure my fame. Like him, it had eluded me and now even the very urge seemed irrelevant or at least unattainable. But with William Canning, the instinct had been reborn (perhaps it had never died) and with his life now drawing surely to a close, I could see it had reached a disturbing intensity. But there was more—the folly of a jealous comparison with an earlier member of the family who had attained just that immortality he craved.

On a sudden impulse, as if to emphasize his point, he began talking about one of his ancestors—William Canynges—one of the great men of Bristol, who in the early fifteenth century had been a famous merchant. From these beginnings, Canynges had gone on to become five times mayor of the city and later its MP. To crown his achievements, he had been instrumental in rebuilding the church of St Mary Redcliffe, one of the most famous churches in the West of England. Here was an ancestor worthy of respect, his achievements within the city, as laudable as they had become immortal. Would that he, William Canning, could also find some work, however humble in comparison, that would ensure that his name lived on.

I listened with interest to his description of William Canynges, though as he returned to his theme of immortality I became increasingly embarrassed once more. But my interest stemmed not so much from the historical details as from a half-forgotten reference to that famous name.

"Canynges!" I said deliberately when he paused, spelling the name as I now recalled where I had seen it before. "Have you ever read 'The Fall of the House of Usher' by Poe?''

Canning was somewhat surprised by the sudden change of conversation.

"I must have read it once," he replied, somewhat bemused.

"There's a reference in that story to a book, *The Mad Trist*, written by a Sir Launcelot Canning. The reference to it, and readings from it, form part of the climax to the story."

My mention of it had been partly casual, a process of thinking out loud once I had discovered the answer to my problem. Now that I thought about it more I remembered from earlier researches on the topic that a number of experts had believed there to be a connection between the mythical Sir Launcelot and William Canynges of Bristol. I found it quite fascinating to be making the acquaintance of a descendant of one who, quite unwittingly, had become part of the Poe legend.

William Canning's own reaction seemed less good-humoured. Perhaps it was because here was yet another aspect of his ancestor's immortality to add to what he already found a depressingly long list. He stood silently as I explained the connection, emphasizing mainly for his benefit the common view, which at the time I shared: the book was purely mythical, an invention of Poe's imagination for the purpose of building up tension in his famous story.

When I had finished William Canning remained silent. He seemed to have become deeply engrossed in his thoughts as if he were recalling some distant event. Then he looked at me.

"*The Mad Trist*. Yes, of course. I had almost forgotten. So long ago."

I did not understand what he meant that night, and he was not willing to elaborate further. Shortly afterwards he left the party, passing me in the corridor as I took my coat to leave. On the steps of Simon Montague's house, only half listening to Simon's garrulous banter, I watched Canning's shuffling figure as it disappeared along the darkly lit street. I wondered then what strange thoughts I had resurrected in him. It was to be several weeks however before I was to get an answer.

*

I did not see him again for some time, not, in fact, until he paid me a call late one evening. He came unannounced and it was so late that I felt sure, as I let him in, that it had to be on the most urgent business. In the event it proved to be a matter that could well have waited, and the meeting served only to confirm in my mind earlier reports of his eccentricity.

He was anxious to know from me the names and addresses of some Poe experts in this country and the United States. At first he would say nothing except that he was researching a short story, but in view of our last meeting I was suspicious. I offered him a drink and was pleased when he finally took off his coat and sat down in front of the fire.

We talked rather casually for a while. I enquired about his book but he seemed to have made no further progress with it. Indeed from his manner it seemed as if he had abandoned it.

After several further drinks, his attitude becoming a good deal more mellow in the process, he mentioned in passing the name of his ancestor William Canynges again. I seized upon it, referring once more to the Poe story, for I felt sure that his enquiry and his famous forebear were linked in some way.

After a short pause during which he seemed to be trying, unsuccessfully as it turned out, to curb his inclination to tell me what he knew, he finally said:

"This life of my illustrious forebear is not quite as honourable as might appear from a superficial account." He paused. "Perhaps I should ask you to keep what I say to yourself, for it is a family legend, you see, that towards the end of his life William Canynges dabbled in the occult. Participating in pagan ceremonies, even founding a clandestine devil-worshipping sect as a result of experiments he had carried out taking drugs. As the legend goes, he was so horrified by what he discovered that he became deeply religious, giving up all secular matters to concentrate his mind on atoning for his blasphemous experiments. That was why he became a monk, shunning all social life until his death in 1474." He paused again. "I remember my father once telling me, goodness that was a long time ago, I had quite forgotten. . .

he once told me that William Canynges had written his experiences down. . .or so it was imagined.''

Canning paused to swallow his drink. I was anxious that he should not leave before he had finished telling me what he knew.

''How is this known?'' I said, topping up his glass.

''Thank you. Oh, it's just handed down the generations. It's a family story.''

For a moment he looked down into his glass. Canning had never married, he had no heirs.

''But what evidence is there of him having written down his experiences? It's a matter of speculation amongst some art historians that drugs were used to induce hypnotic trances, and these visions then provided ideas for some Renaissance painters. There's Hieronymus Bosch, for example. But the paintings exist. Was any manuscript ever found?''

Canning smiled.

''It's true,'' he went on, ''that no trace of a book or even a manuscript was ever found amongst Canynges's papers and possessions. But that's not quite the end of the matter.''

Canning leant forward, lowering his voice as if afraid that his words might be overheard by some unseen but malevolent force.

''On his deathbed, Canynges is supposed to have given the book to one of the monks. Apparently his illness was sudden and in his dying moments he pleaded with the man to destroy the book. Now, for one reason or another, the monk is supposed not to have obeyed these instructions. Maybe he read it and would not take the responsibility for burning it. Whatever the reason, he kept it in his possession for over a quarter of a century and then in his turn entrusted it to another priest who was sailing from Bristol to America with John Cabot. Perhaps in some way he felt he was fulfilling his pledge to William, for he must have thought that once in America it would be lost forever.''

Canning sat back in his chair as if the effort of recounting the tale had exhausted him. He stared at me, and I can still recall those haunting eyes, for he was like a man who had sensed his mission in life. A current of excitement ran through everything he said.

"The book did reach America, according to the family story, but what happened to it after that no one knows." He paused, continuing with a note of triumph in his voice. "The book remained lost until Poe himself saw it."

"Poe!" I exclaimed. It took me a second to realize what he was saying. "You mean that book, the one William Canynges wrote of his experiences, was *The Mad Trist* in 'The Fall of the House of Usher?'"

"Exactly!" said Canning. "I believe that there was such a book, and that it is no chance that the names of Sir Launcelot Canning and William Canynges are linked. They are one and the same!"

"But the book is mythical," I protested.

"Correction. It is believed to be mythical. I tell you that such a book was written, and I believe Poe saw a copy of it and used it in his story."

I was amazed by his suggestion. Coming from anyone else I would have dismissed it as mere idle speculation, but coming from a descendant of the man, it had to be taken seriously even though it ran counter to everything that was known about Poe's reference to *The Mad Trist*. Indeed the revelation—if it were true—threw a new and fascinating light not only on the story, but also on Poe's life itself. Was it possible, for example, that the depravities supposedly contained therein had been partly to blame for Poe's own disintegration of mind and his own descent into alcohol and drugs? Was it possible that the terrors described in the Canynges manuscript, only hinted at in 'The Fall of the House of Usher', really existed in some lost manuscript? What an incredible discovery it would make! What a sensation it would create in literary and occult circles! What immortality it would create for the man who discovered the manuscript!

Immortality! I looked up at him and realized that the very idea had occurred to him. Why else would he have given up work on his novel? Now he was standing and his words carried a deep and disturbing conviction:

"And now, if you please, I would be obliged if you would give

me those addresses, for I have work to do. I hope I can trust to
your discretion in this matter. It would not do to reveal any of this
until more definite proof can be presented.''

And there the matter rested for several weeks, at least as far as I
was concerned. I must confess that the thought of discovering
such a rare and important document fascinated me even then, but
I did nothing, nor could I discover what progress Canning was
making. I did not see him, and though I passed his house on
several occasions it always seemed deserted.

As it happened I met him again, quite by chance, one Friday
night. I had gone to a little restaurant near the dockland section of
Bristol. It is my habit to dine out once a week to escape the mono-
tony of my own cooking. As fate would have it on that occasion
he was there and though he seemed none too pleased, I managed
to invite myself to his table.

It took little effort on my part to turn the conversation towards
his quest for *The Mad Trist* though as before he seemed reluctant
to go into detail. Remembering our earlier conversation and the
lubricating effect liquor seemed to have upon him I ordered a
bottle of wine and duly began to ply the man. Yet for all he said
that night it seemed to me at the time that he had made little
progress. Little did I realize that, in a way, the discoveries he had
already made had sealed his terrible fate.

''I cannot help wondering if there is a clue in the life of this
gentleman.''

Canning had been visiting the church of St Mary Redcliffe, his
ancestor's crowning achievement. From conversations he had
had, he had made a connection between his illustrious forebear
and the celebrated Bristol poet Thomas Chatterton. The connection could hardly have been more bizarre.

Canning explained that Chatterton had lived some three
hundred years after William Canynges. Moreover, whereas
Canynges had found status and distinction in his time, Chatterton's brief life—a mere eighteen years—had been marked as

much by scandal as by any honourable recognition. He had indulged in literary fraud, fabricating "antique" verses and plays. He had gained further notoriety by satirizing leading figures of Bristol. Partly because of this he had left Bristol in 1770 and come to London, lodging first in Shoreditch later in Holborn. Although he had some further literary success, it provided insufficient reward to prevent him from descending into the ranks of the penniless and starving. Finally, in despair, he committed suicide, so ending his days in a pauper's grave attached to the Shoe Lane Workhouse. Not until after his death did collections of his work appear in print.

I could not imagine how the lives of two such different men could in any way be connected. Canning however was obviously enjoying my confusion and he savoured the explanation like a detective confronting a murderer with the weight of damning evidence.

"Chatterton claimed in 1768 to have found a manuscript written by Canynges. It was entitled 'Elinour and Juga', but, and this is the real point. . .he claimed to have found the manuscript in Canynges's coffin in St Mary Redcliffe."

Canning sat back to observe my reaction. In the event I must have disappointed him.

"Claimed?" I queried. "What do you mean? Does this manuscript exist?"

Canning seemed offended by my question and after a rather lengthy silence he replied testily, "Well, the manuscript was probably a forgery. Chatterton is thought to have written it himself."

I said nothing in reply and his manner became more indignant. But how could I react otherwise? It seemed to me he was behaving irrationally. In the absence of any solid evidence he was grabbing at anything. If the manuscript was a forgery, whether Chatterton claimed it came from Canynges's coffer was of little significance. If the "Elinour and Juga" manuscript was genuine, did he seriously believe that *The Mad Trist* or a copy of it might lie in the same place in Canynges's tomb? Surely if it did exist, the notorious Chatterton would have taken that manuscript too. And yet, I reflected, there was the young poet's suicide to consider. Was it possible that the text was so horrific that he had returned it to the tomb? Was it possible that what the book revealed played some part in Chatterton's eventual suicide, as perhaps it did in Poe's own death? The coincidence was striking.

I was about to ask him whether that was his belief but the chance was lost as he said,

"And there's this as well." His voice carried an undercurrent of hostility now. He was finding my attitude tedious.

He took out of his pocket a letter that had come from America. Presumably one of my American contacts had been able to give him something. He unfolded a small piece of paper and handed it across to me. It was a photocopy of a page from an old newspaper, *The Saturday Museum*. Poe had been associated with it in 1843, but the piece here made yet another reference to the mysterious Sir Launcelot Canning. The story referred to a publication Poe had been planning to start called *The Stylus*. For his motto, Poe had planned to use a quote signed with the name Launcelot Canning. I read it, and then re-read it, making little sense of its message:

> —— unbending that all men
> Of thy firm TRUTH may say—"Lo! this is writ
>   With the antique *iron* pen."

I handed it back to him, shrugging my shoulders in a display of incomprehension.

"I had hoped you would have been more. . .open minded."

Canning was obviously offended. He had mistaken my gesture for a form of ridicule. It had not been intended as such, simply a sign that I did not understand the importance of these fragmented pieces of information. It was too late however to undo the damage and he looked at me fiercely as he stood up to leave.

"I am sorry that you consider my efforts wasted and the results of my research nothing more than meaningless bits of gibberish."

I could feel in his voice all the hurt pride of a man who had suffered countless rejections from others he took to be less talented or less worthy than himself. He pulled on his coat hurriedly. There was no arrogance in his movements, no sense of inner conviction that could not be destroyed by an indifferent world. His manner was more transparent than that. He was like a hurt child whose first faltering efforts had met a stern rebuke. He wanted to be away from me and any attempt on my part to repair the damage would only have added insult to the wreck of our brief confidence.

In the distance the small group of mourners had begun to move away from the graveside. I stood upright now, no longer leaning against the yew tree. I wanted to walk over to the grave, but I felt a hand rest on my shoulder.

"Please go on," whispered my companion. "I am sure you have more to tell me."

The story was nearly told, but the most important pieces were still missing. Now that I had started, it was only right to finish.

In the days that followed I became obsessed by what Canning had told me. Nothing of what he had said had really made sense, and yet nor was I able to dismiss his words from my mind. Perhaps his own intensity had something to do with it, the evident fervour with which he was pursuing his enquiries. Looking back, perhaps that was the only thread that ran through this whole business, but it was enough to draw me one day down to the church of St Mary Redcliffe—that and a phone call I had just had from Simon Montague, telling me that Canning had been making regular visits to the church, spending long hours in silent contemplation near Canynges's tomb. I was reminded of course of our last conversation. Here surely was the answer to the question I had been unable to put to him. Canning really did believe that some part of the mystery had its solution in the tomb of William Canynges. Was it concern for his safety or some less honourable motive that encouraged me to find out more about what he was doing?

On my first visit I managed to speak to one of the wardens of the church. He had, in fact, noticed Canning, his attention having been drawn by a number of sudden outbursts. Canning, it seemed, on more than one occasion, had ended his vigil in a state of some agitation, roaring incoherently at his ancestor's tomb before storming out of the church in a fury.

I made no reference to any of the conversations I had had with Canning. I certainly could not be sure he was about to make some dramatic move, and yet on an impulse I described myself to the warden as a close friend. I suggested to him that if Canning began acting strangely again that he might care to let me know. I told him that the old man had no close relations and rather than let the police deal with any odd behaviour, I would do my best to intercede. I indicated to him that his behaviour was just one aspect of encroaching senility. I left him with my telephone number.

Two weeks passed and nothing happened. Then late one evening, whilst I was at home working, the phone rang. It was a call from the church warden of St Mary Redcliffe. He sounded anxious and begged me to come immediately; if not, his only recourse would be to call in the police. William Canning had somehow got into the muniment room where his ancestor's remains lay buried and had now barricaded himself in. Strange noises were coming from the room. I told the warden I would be there immediately, yet even as I hurried to make the appointment I could not in any way imagine the reason for William Canning's strange turn of behaviour.

I arrived to find the warden waiting for me at the North Porch and we went immediately to the door of the muniment room. Even as we approached the solid oak door, we could both hear the strange incantations issuing from within. The words were incoherent, but the strangely guttural tones had a pagan quality. I thought of desecration, for it was as if the very presence of these sounds was offensive, an abomination to the surroundings in which they were uttered.

"Mr Canning." The warden beat on the oak door, as if to

demonstrate the nature of his earlier efforts. It was clear that such exertion was futile.

"What could he be using," I asked, "to barricade himself in?"

"There are some chairs in there, and a table. Nothing else except a visitor's book and pen."

"Then should we push? Perhaps if we both try we might get in."

Judging by the sounds coming from within it seemed imperative that we act quickly.

The warden nodded and we both leant our weight hard against the door. But even as we did so, the sounds from within seemed to rise to a new and terrifying crescendo. We pushed harder and felt something behind the door slip. As the door gave an inch a thin stream of light cut the cloistered gloom and the sounds rose to yet a new climax. A thin column of incense curled out through the slit in the door. Even in that poor light I could see that the interior was heavily laden with smoke.

"More!" I shouted and we heaved again. The door gave another inch and through the murk I could see a figure moving slowly about the room, his arms held up aloft whilst strange inhuman sounds seemed to pour from his barely opened mouth.

"Canning!" I shouted, for in that instant I feared for his life. What was it that made me predict so accurately that within that terrible place, Canning was stirring up forces far beyond his capacity to contain? Was it perhaps that I sensed Canning was not alone?

I shouted to him again as we moved the obstruction further back, but still I could not gain access and now it seemed as if he were screaming the words. Yet why did his lips not move? It was as if he were possessed, not the master of the rites he was performing, but in some strange way the sacrificial victim.

"Canning! Stop before it is too late!"

We pushed again, harder still, and yet with every slight movement of the door it seemed as if Canning's figure was retreating further into the thick smoke at the far end of the room. The smoke descended like a shroud and a shrill scream broke the air.

Was it Canning's voice? His figure was now lost.

"Canning, for God's sake!"

In that instant the obstruction gave and we staggered into the room. Canning was before us, half enveloped in the gloom, his body now seeming to be above us, as if elevated by some giant hand.

"The tomb! The tomb!"

Canning, his face transfixed, seemed to be pointing at his ancestor's tomb. Had he made the discovery? Had he found out where the manuscript lay? But as he moved towards me I could see that his hand was clutching his heart. He staggered, his foot catching a large book that lay open on the floor near the centre of the room.

I rushed towards him, grabbing him as he fell and then laying him gently on the ground. As I did so I saw that the stone flags were covered with strange symbols.

But in that moment I realized Canning was dead and as I moved his hand I could see that he had been clutching a pen—an ancient rusted iron pen that had been driven into his body.

"The visitor's pen," gasped the warden.

"The antique iron pen!" Now words that had seemed so incomprehensible before returned to my mind. They were no more comprehensible now and yet they carried a bitter irony:

> —— unbending that all men
> Of thy firm TRUTH may say—"Lo! this is writ
>   With the antique *iron* pen."

I looked up at the warden. I made no mention of what I knew, but instead recalled an earlier sensation just before we had entered the muniment room.

"There is no one in this room except you and I. But look!"

I showed him how deeply the lethal point had been driven into Canning's body, and then added: "Could he possibly have done this himself?"

In that moment I saw the book that Canning had tripped on.

I pulled it towards me across the floor and after scanning the text turned to the title page.

"The book," I said to my companion, "was by the necromancer Dr John Dee. Canning had been using one of his occult books to resurrect the ghost of his ancestor either to point the way conclusively to the tomb where he believed the book to be, or else to tell him where it did lie. If he discovered anything, then his message died with him."

My companion said nothing, but I felt his presence behind me as I walked slowly towards the freshly dug grave. The gravedigger was near by, preparing to do his work.

"I cannot help but wonder," I continued, "whether in the end Canning was right."

"What do you mean?" he asked.

"His last words, his last gestures were to point to the tomb. I cannot help wondering if in the end the old man was right—the manuscript, or some copy of it, does lie in the tomb."

The idea had been preying on my mind ever since the night of Canning's ceremony.

We were standing beside the grave of William Canning now, and as I took a small handful of dirt and sprinkled it onto the wooden coffin, I added:

"Immortality. It is a futile quest of itself, but when the fruit is there for the picking. . ."

"So you too are fascinated by the same possibility?"

I sensed that my companion's voice had changed. . .had stiffened. For the first time he walked past me and stood staring at me from the far side of the grave, his eyes almost luminous in the gloom that had now descended on the graveyard. A cold wind was rising, gusting about me yet somehow not disturbing the stillness that had also suddenly fallen.

I looked away, unable to return his remorseless gaze. The gravedigger, who was standing near us, seemed transfixed, his hand upon the spade. In the distance the mourners were motionless. It was as if time itself had stopped.

Immediately I looked back at my companion, whose head was now bowed as if in silent supplication. His appearance had changed too. Now he was standing before me in monk's habit so that even as he raised his head, the long cowl hid every feature of his face. Even before he spoke I now knew who my companion was. Canning's ceremony had not failed in its intended purpose. I had not been deceived in those moments before entering the muniment room.

"Why do you crave immortality at my expense? You must pursue this matter no further!"

His voice was threatening and as he spoke he held out his fist, as if he were holding a knife, and then brought it down with a sudden jabbing motion. The gesture could only have been a re-enactment of how that murderous antique iron pen had been driven into Canning's heart. As I had first suspected, that fatal wound had not been self-inflicted, and now before me stood Canning's murderer.

"Then tell me where it is? Where is *The Mad Trist*?"

At last I spoke the words. Even if this were to be my final hour and the knowledge of that book to be the instrument of my destruction, yet still, like Canning before me, I wanted to know. Like one who wishes to know the profoundest mysteries of the universe, in that instant I would have sacrificed my life for a moment of truth.

The sounds echoed through the stillness of the graveyard as I repeated:

"Tell me where the book is to be found and I swear to God I will say nothing. Is it in the tomb?"

He started to move away now, melting into the darkness, but then paused as if he could not decide whether to give me an answer. I begged him again and he turned to face me.

"Is it in the tomb?" I repeated. "Tell me!"

"You are correct, for where else could it be. . ." His words were barely audible, as if they were addressed as much to himself as to me. I sensed a riddle in what he said and as he spoke he lowered his cowl so that for the first time I saw his face.

In that moment before he was lost to my sight I understood his meaning more clearly than if it had been inscribed on parchment and set before me. For was not every page of that "book" etched upon his tortured face? Was not every word reflected in his haunted eyes? Here was the true object of that fatal quest, as perhaps Canning had realized in his last seconds of life. For me Canynges's message stretched out through time to speak more eloquently than any text, indeed it was a message that Poe himself would have understood well: What need have they of a book—those who have spoken with the Devil.

FOUR CLASSIC POE STORIES

"The Murders in the Rue Morgue" (1841)
Illustration by Charles Mackay.

"The Masque of the Red Death" (1842)
Illustration by Aubrey Beardsley

"The Pit and the Pendulum" (1843)
Illustration by Arthur Rackham

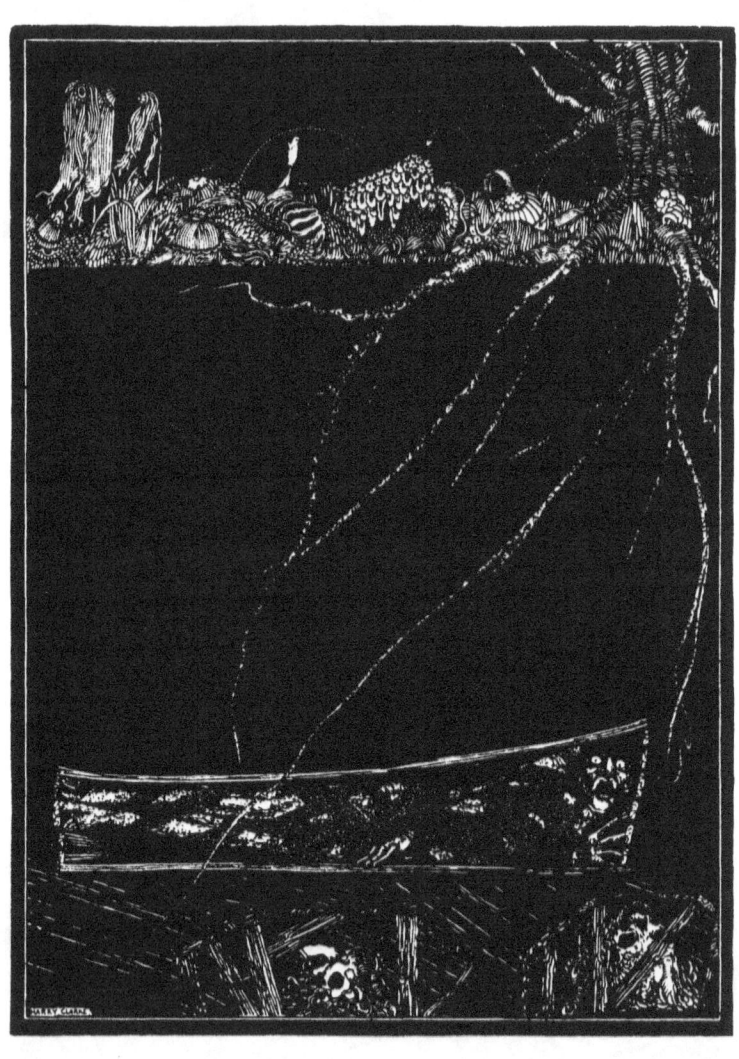

"The Premature Burial" (1844)
Illustration by Harry Clarke